SHELF-MADE MAN

KIM FIELDING

Tin Box
— PRESS —

For Joel Leslie, who gifted me the plot bunny and title, and who has so often dazzled me by bringing my stories to life.

CHAPTER
ONE

The lobby gave Tobias Lykke an instant headache.

The space had obviously been very grand seventy years ago, but the grandeur had been allowed to fade. Someone had more recently made a half-baked effort at a more hip and urban décor, and now Christmas baubles had been added to the mix in what appeared to be a completely random fashion.

The concierge, who might have been the party responsible for some of the decorating disaster, peered at Tobias with lowered brow. "Can I help you?"

"I, uh...." Tobias tried to shrink in on himself in hopes of looking less threatening, but since he was over six feet tall and hefty, he knew it was a lost cause. "I'm here to see Virginia Segreti."

"You mean the Countess of Contovello."

"She's not really— Yes, the Countess."

"The Countess does not receive visitors." Apparently the concierge had been a royal bodyguard in a previous life. Must be quite a comedown to end up as desk staff in a condominium.

"But she asked me to come. She's my aunt." Although the latter wasn't really the concierge's business—and also wasn't strictly accurate—Tobias thought it gave him a little extra cred.

After a pause, the concierge picked up a phone handset. "Just a moment." He poked some buttons, then turned away and murmured into the receiver as if transmitting state secrets.

"Apartment 14C," he said grudgingly after he'd hung up.

"I know. I've been here before." It had been a long time, however.

The elevator interior was mirrored, which gave Tobias a chance to check his hair and tie. On the very few occasions when his aunt deigned to have a visitor, she insisted they dress up. He supposed he should be grateful that she didn't make him rent a tux. Anyway, since his suit—the only one he owned—fit okay, his tie was straight, and his hair was mostly behaving itself, he'd probably pass inspection, even though he always felt ridiculous when dressed like this.

Apartment 14C was at the end of the hallway. He stood outside the door for a long moment, took a deep breath, and knocked.

A voice came from inside. "Tobias? Do enter." Although he knew very well that she had been born and raised in Southern California, her accent tended to waver somewhere between Katharine Hepburn and Queen Elizabeth II.

He stepped into a small foyer with ornate floral wallpaper and a carved wooden table with a marble top. The last time he'd been here—ten years ago—an oval mirror in a gilded frame had hung over the table. Now only a ghostly image remained where the wallpaper was less faded.

"In here, boy!"

The room that she insisted on calling the parlor was mostly dark, and the heavy scent of fresh gardenias didn't entirely mask the odor of musty old furniture. The heavy curtains were closed against the sunny day, and a single dim lamp—set on a table in the center of the room—barely illuminated the deep burgundy walls. Even though he couldn't clearly see the many paintings that hung on the walls, he knew from past experience that they all featured a beautiful young woman.

"Well, look at you! Haven't you become a fine young man."

She was seated in an armchair in the darkest corner of the room, barely discernible in her long black dress. All he could make out was her curled blonde hair, which had to be a wig.

"Thank you for inviting me, my lady."

She laughed musically. "Oh, you can call me Aunt Virginia. You know that."

Technically, she wasn't his aunt. She'd been his

grandmother's closest childhood friend and had always referred to his mother as her niece. When Tobias came along, he became her godson and honorary nephew. He didn't mind, especially now that neither of them had any remaining relatives.

Tobias lifted the fancy paper shopping bag clutched in his hand. "I brought you a little something." It was a box of her favorite teas, which he'd ordered online from a shop in Singapore, and her favorite chocolates, shipped from Italy. His credit card bill had suffered, but he didn't want to skimp on Aunt Virginia.

"You're such a good boy. You can place the bag on the table there." A spectral pale hand gestured. "Now, do you need to use the restroom, darling?"

He blushed. "No, thank you." When he was five or six, his mother had brought him here on a visit shortly after he'd downed a lunchtime can of Coke. He'd nearly wet his pants, which Aunt Virginia never seemed to forget, even though his thirtieth birthday had come and gone.

"Well, have a seat." Her hand motioned toward a chair halfway across the room from her.

Hoping he wouldn't crash into any unseen furniture along the way, Tobias made his way to the wooden chair, tall-backed and with heavy carved arms and a barely cushioned seat. It felt like something that would be used in the early stages of an interrogation by the Inquisition—the next step being the rack. At least he didn't have to worry whether the sturdy chair would support his bulk.

"Thank you for coming to visit an old lady. I know from your letters that your work keeps you very busy."

"Ma'am, I always have time for your delightful company." Even though he didn't affect a sophisticated accent, whenever he spoke to her—in person or in writing—he found himself sounding as if he'd stepped out of a Victorian novel. He had to make a concerted effort to sound normal.

Her skirts rustled as if she were smoothing them. "I do quite enjoy our correspondence, and I'm impressed by your faithfulness with it. Few young people would bother to write to an old lady at all, let alone several times per year. I believe, in fact, that your generation relies entirely on electronic communication, and that is a shame. Elegant handwriting on fine paper is so much more meaningful. It's the personal touch, you know. One lingers over a handwritten letter."

Tobias smiled. "I enjoy getting mail from you too." That was entirely true. Whenever one of her cream-colored envelopes arrived, his day improved dramatically. He liked running his fingers over the thick paper, carefully opening the flap, and drawing out the hand-tinted card with the embossed eagle. She usually gave him a short anecdote about some famous person she'd once met—now long dead—followed by some general advice. Her handwriting was impeccable. The best thing was knowing that someone had taken the time and effort to reach out to him.

"When I was younger, I used to entertain often. But

now, well, you know I've become a bit of a recluse and my visitors are rare."

"I'm honored you invited me."

"I did so because I have something I would like to give you. Oh, don't get too excited. My estate will go to charity. The Museum of Modern Art can take whatever they want, and the remainder will go to the Global Women's Fund."

"I didn't— That's all very far in the future anyway."

She laughed. "You're sweet."

He honestly hadn't even thought about a potential inheritance from her, and now, even though she must be in her nineties, he found the idea of her death quite distressing. His link to her might be rather tenuous, but she was all he had left.

"Stay here," she said. "I'll go fetch it." There was more skirt rustling before a door creaked open, admitting a sliver of light, and then she was gone.

That left Tobias shifting uncomfortably on the torture chair and trying to get a better view of the room's contents, now that his eyes had adjusted. As far as he could tell, nothing had changed since he'd last been here, which was the December after he graduated college—an entire decade ago.

He didn't know whether Aunt Virginia was, in fact, a member of the nobility. She claimed that her deceased fourth and final husband had been an Italian count. Of course, she also claimed that her third husband was a 1950s movie star who she was forbidden by the divorce agreement to name, and that her second husband was a wizard who was eventually and unwillingly dragged to another dimension. So Tobias took her title with a grain of salt, although he never expressed his disbelief aloud.

On the other hand, her first husband was a well-known artist. That he knew to be true because the guy, who'd been a couple of decades her senior when she married at eighteen, had created all those paintings of her. Tobias's mother had told him that some of them hung in art museums, which had impressed him even when he was a child.

Regardless of whether she was truly a countess, it didn't hurt to behave as if she were. It made her happy, anyway.

Aunt Virginia returned several minutes later. He caught a glimpse of her when the door opened, and she appeared to be carrying a shoebox. Then she closed the door and returned to her chair.

"You know, Tobias, in your letters you speak a good deal about your work. But what about your personal life? Are you dating someone, perhaps?"

He was glad she couldn't see him wince. "Not really." There were hookups now and then, but most of them proved disappointing.

"Surely there must be many eligible young men in Portland. Are they too foolish to see your value?"

"I guess I just haven't clicked with anyone. But it's okay. Work keeps me busy, and—"

"Yes." There was a tapping that sounded like her fingers on cardboard. "When I was a young woman, I had so many adventures. You can't even imagine them all. And in between husbands, I had dozens of lovers. Mostly men, although some lovely women as well. Ah, it was wonderful."

She paused as if to allow this to sink in. He'd always known her as an old woman who dressed beautifully but kept herself tucked away in her apartment. His mother once told him that if Aunt Virginia went out, she did so at night. It had never occurred to Tobias that she might have been pretty wild during her youth. Although maybe the nude paintings on her walls should have been a clue.

When she continued, she wounded wistful. "I settled down when I married *il conte*, of course. He was such a fine man. Very kind and intelligent—and ten years my junior. I thought we'd have the rest of our lives together. But alas, he grew ill, and... and our time was cut short. By the time I had mourned enough and was ready to continue my life, I was well past the flower of youth. I was no longer the girl people admired in paintings."

"But—"

"Hush. Let me finish. I withdrew, Toby. I could not face the world with my wrinkles and gray hair, so I tucked myself away. The older I became, the deeper I burrowed. Until now, when so few days remain to me and I find myself entirely unable to unlock the cage I've put myself in."

Tobias's throat felt tight. "But you're such a fascinating person, my lady. I've never met anyone as interesting as you. It's a shame to deny the world your company. I'd be happy to escort you anywhere you wish."

"Oh, you are a dear boy, but it's simply no longer possible. Do not fret, however. I have made peace with it. I only mention it because I am afraid you are locking yourself away as well, and you're far too young and vital for this. Carpe diem, gather ye rosebuds, or as your generation likes to say, YOLO."

"I, um...." Tobias didn't know how to respond to this. She was correct that he'd been fairly hermity, and not by choice. Unlike her, though, he was no beauty. He was weird, and pretty boring, and had a really hard time connecting with people. He'd never had many friends as a child, instead being the type of kid who spent recesses sitting against a wall and reading a book, pretending he didn't mind that nobody wanted to play with him.

"You deserve happiness," Aunt Virginia said. "If you're happy alone and at home, that's perfectly fine. But if you're not, don't wait too long to change things, dear. The years slip by faster than you think." She stood, skirts rustling, and set the box on the lamp table, then returned to her seat.

"Thank you for caring about me," Tobias said, meaning it. He didn't tell her that he had no clue how to follow her advice.

"I'm afraid that I must end our visit. You came all

this way to see me, and you are such a delight, but I'm ancient and I tire easily."

He stood quickly. "Of course. My lady, is there anything I can do for you? Errands? Things that need fixing?"

"I'm quite set, my dear boy, but it's very kind of you to ask. Please take your box before you go."

By now his eyes had adapted to the dark, and although he still couldn't see her well, he made it to the table without tripping over anything. He picked up the box and tucked it under one arm.

"Don't open it until you get home."

He suppressed a groan. That was over six hundred miles. His curiosity was going to kill him. "Okay."

"Oh, and one more thing. Do you have plans for Christmas?"

"Would you like to spend it together?" he asked, surprised. It was only a week away, and they hadn't spent the holidays together since he was a boy.

"I prefer to celebrate alone, thank you. I merely wished to point out that at some points in the year, the border between the possible and the impossible becomes more permeable. The later part of December —with the Solstice and Christmas—is one of those times. My second husband and I used to... well, perhaps those memories are better kept to myself." She chuckled. "It's a good time to be daring, Tobias. To try something new."

Now he was just confused. Maybe being tired was making her confused too. But he thanked her nonetheless, and she thanked him for visiting and for the gift he'd brought, and then he let himself out.

In the elevator on the way down, it felt as if something shifted inside the box, and he nearly opened it. But he'd promised to wait.

TWO

T obias was taking Amtrak home. He always found it uncomfortable to be crammed into an airplane seat for any amount of time, and the scenery along the train's route between San Francisco and Portland was supposed to be beautiful. Unfortunately, it was already dark by the time he boarded in Emeryville. He slept poorly on the too-small train mattress, despite having sprung for a roomette, and was bleary-eyed by the time the sun rose somewhere near Klamath Falls, Oregon. When he finally stumbled into his little bungalow, it was almost dinnertime and all he wanted to do was eat, shower, and fall into bed.

He felt slightly guilty for putting off the huge pile of work that awaited him. But he'd planned to work through Christmas anyway, and that would make up for these two days away.

He'd already rooted through his freezer, unearthed

one of the frozen meals he'd picked up during his last Trader Joe's run, and started up the microwave when he remembered the box. It was right there in his tiny living room, perched on the love seat where he'd dropped his things when exhaustion and hunger distracted him.

Now, as the microwave whirred away, he wandered into the living room and picked up the box—old and worn, as if it had been tucked away in a closet for a long time. Its weight felt as if there might still be a pair of shoes inside, but that in itself was puzzling. Tobias supposed it could be shoes from one of Aunt Virginia's previous husbands, but he couldn't figure out why she would be gifting them.

Well, there was no point in mulling over the contents when he could simply take a look. The lid was attached with yellowed tape, which he carefully peeled away. When he opened the box he discovered a lumpy object wrapped in cloth. He lifted it out, set the box aside, and peered at the cloth. The cobalt fabric was thick and lustrous, embroidered in silver thread with stylized snowflakes. Silk brocade, he guessed. It had probably cost a fortune. But he also guessed that the focus was supposed to be on whatever it encased.

Very gingerly he unrolled the fabric and found... a doll.

Not a baby doll or a Barbie, however. Actually, maybe *figurine* was a better term, because this seemed like the sort of object intended for display rather than for a child to play with. It was about a foot tall, with jointed shoulders, elbows, hips, and knees, which had allowed it to fit in the box. The face, hair, and body were made of finely painted porcelain, and its clothing and hat were made of velvet and lace.

It was, in fact, a Christmas elf, with a peaked cap, red tunic, and green-and-white striped stockings. It had yellow hair and blue eyes, and Tobias thought its smile was more sweet than mischievous.

The elf was adorable, although Tobias was disappointed that there was some damage to one leg: the fabric torn and the porcelain underneath cracked.

Well, it would still be nice as a holiday decoration. Tobias set it on the bookshelf in front of his collection of old sci-fi paperbacks, where it looked... festive, he supposed. He hadn't bothered with any other holiday décor.

When he checked the box, he saw that it also contained a folded sheet of paper, thick but yellowed and somewhat brittle. The inside contained a note written in spidery, old-fashioned cursive, which Tobias had a little trouble deciphering.

I have protected him for now, but unfortunately I am unable to restore him to his proper state. Please care for him well.

—Olve Lange

Tobias was fairly certain that had been the name of Aunt Virginia's second husband, the wizard. The elf must have belonged to him. Tobias didn't know why Aunt Virginia had decided to give it to him, but the elf must have been treasured, so he appreciated her thoughtfulness.

"Thanks, Aunt Virginia," he said aloud. He'd write her a letter, perhaps tomorrow, after he'd tackled some of the work backlog.

Then he returned to the kitchen, where the microwave beeped impatiently.

TOBIAS WOKE up early the next day—Friday—yawned through a cup of coffee and slice of toast, and then tackled his email inbox. One good thing about his data engineer job was that he could do a lot of work from home. And on a day like today, when he had no meetings, he could do it in flannel pajamas and a ratty but comfy sweatshirt he'd owned since college. The flip side of that, however, was that he didn't have contact with many people outside of formal business interactions. Sure, there was a lot of electronic discussion with stakeholders and clients, and endless Zooms, and even times when he met up with people in person. But during those times, the conversation centered pretty exclusively on work. There was none of the chitchat that might lead to making friends.

He'd had a hard enough time making social connections as a kid, but it turned out to be even more difficult in adulthood. His hobbies—reading, Legos, wandering in forests—tended to be solitary. His neighbors were pleasant but he didn't seem to have much in common with them aside from living on the same block. Bars and clubs made him feel so awkward and nervous that he literally broke out in hives. His only family was Aunt Virginia, and she'd been a recluse for decades.

So he worked. Luckily, he loved his job. All those predictable equations and cozy lines of code, and when he solved a problem, when he made it easier for a client to collect and analyze data, that was incredibly satisfying.

Mostly.

But now that Christmas was almost upon him and work was pretty much his only agenda item? That was a little disheartening.

On Friday he kept himself chained to the computer until nearly dinnertime, at which point he went for a long run. If you could call it that; he'd briefly dated a guy who referred to Tobias's exercise attempts as *plodding*. Thanks to long legs, Tobias could cover a lot of ground, but he wasn't speedy about it. Today was damp, and he sloshed through puddles and dealt with a runny nose and avoided getting run over by impatient drivers eager to get home for the weekend. He took a different route every time he went out, rarely paying conscious attention to his twists and turns. He'd been blessed with an excellent sense of direction and had no trouble finding his way home. Today when he returned to his bungalow, he took a hot shower and nuked Korean food from Trader Joe's.

He considered doing more work after dinner but

vetoed the idea, instead penning a thank-you note to Aunt Virginia. Afterward he watched *Midsomer Murders* while working on the ridiculously expensive Star Wars Lego kit he'd bought himself as a Christmas gift. Interspersed with the construction, he nibbled on the cannabis-infused snickerdoodle he'd purchased before visiting Aunt Virginia. He rarely indulged in mind-altering substances, but now and then a little THC helped him relax. Combining it with Lego probably wasn't a good idea, however; his Millennium Falcon was now looking decidedly unspaceworthy.

Finally he decided to call it a night. As he shuffled past the bookshelf, he paused to stare at the elf, whose painted eyes had been watching him all night. "You're pretty quiet, but you're the best company I've had in ages," Tobias informed it blearily. "Really, you're the *only* company I've had in ages."

The elf looked back at him, eyes wide, smile maybe a touch wistful.

Tobias gently stroked the place where the elf was damaged, wondering whether he could get it repaired somewhere in town. After the holidays, maybe. "I wish we really could talk to each other," he said with a sigh. "I wish you were real."

A spell of dizziness hit him hard, and the room seemed to tilt and shift. He clutched his head. "Too much snickerdoodle."

And he staggered off to bed.

~

ONE BENEFIT of cannabis over alcohol was that he didn't wake up hungover. In fact, on Saturday morning he felt good enough that he went for a long run, followed by a soothing shower, and then out again for coffee and brunch at a nearby café. He ate there a couple of times a month and knew the waitstaff fairly well. He'd even gone on a few dates with one of them the previous year. He and Jayden had mutually agreed that the chemistry wasn't right for romance, and they might have become friends if Jayden hadn't gotten accepted to grad school in Boston. A friendship over before it had truly begun.

On a happier note, the café had amazing french toast.

It was gray today but not raining, and Tobias took his time strolling home. He admired the sculptural shapes of trees against the leaden sky, the front yard greenery persisting despite the season, and the architectural details on the century-old houses. He mulled over the idea of a vacation in February, when work tended to be a bit slow and the winter felt endless. It had been a few years since he'd taken more than a couple of days off, and aside from the recent visit to Aunt Virginia, he'd rarely gone farther than the eighty miles it took to reach the coast. As he neared his house, he tried to picture himself sitting on a beach chair, book in his lap and umbrella drink close at hand, the salty breeze rustling his hair. Well, maybe not. That wasn't exactly his style. But he could go hiking somewhere that had warm winters.

He entered the house through the side door because it led into a small mudroom where he could hang his coat and take off his soggy sneakers and socks. He slipped on a pair of dry socks, then went directly into the kitchen and considered whether he wanted a cup of tea.

Something crashed in the living room.

Tobias dashed through the dining room toward the sound, his stockinged feet almost sliding out from underneath him on the wood floor. He skidded like a cartoon character when he took the corner.

"Ahhh!"

It was unclear who screamed louder: Tobias or the stranger huddled on the floor.

But Tobias moved first, striding forward and trying to look as big as possible, as if he were confronting a grizzly bear instead of a terrified man wearing a tunic and striped stockings. Tobias was aware that his height caused him to tower over others. And he wasn't exactly lean, because he liked carbs even more than running. He'd been informed that he had Resting Bitch Face and tended to look intimidating, which certainly didn't help in his quest for new friends. Of course, now he wasn't resting and his expression was probably a combination of anger and shock, but the principle remained.

"Who are you?" Tobias roared. He didn't have anything near at hand to use as a weapon, but it appeared as if the intruder was also unarmed.

The man curled into a fetal ball, arms over his face, and said, "No, please no."

That brought Tobias to a sudden halt, as did his realization that the man was injured. Bright blood stained his leg and was forming a small puddle on the floor. A wave of dizziness hit Tobias at the sight of it, and he growled at himself to focus on the real emergency instead of giving in to a stupid phobia.

Had the man cut himself breaking in? Tobias glanced around, but as far as he could tell the windows were intact and the front door was closed and chained. There were no signs of intrusion at all, except for the intruder himself.

It occurred to Tobias that a 911 call was in order. But he'd left his phone in the kitchen and wasn't inclined to let the bleeding stranger out of his sight. He couldn't just stand there like a dumb statue either, of course. So, feigning confidence and control, he stomped closer. "Who are you?" he demanded. "What are you doing here?"

The man simply cowered.

After another moment of hesitation—and a lurch in his stomach due to the blood—Tobias knelt beside him. "Hey," he said, and touched the man's shoulder.

"No!" The man scrambled away and tried to get to his feet but cried out and collapsed again. "Please don't," he rasped when Tobias carefully approached.

While Tobias was still experiencing a maelstrom of emotions, and while the blood was still mighty unsettling, his concern for the terrified stranger was now foremost. As far as Tobias could tell, he had no weapon and certainly didn't look as if he could physically over-power Tobias. Not only was he injured, but he was also shorter than Tobias and much more slight. *Delicate* was the descriptor that came to mind.

Tobias crept closer but this time didn't try to touch. He spoke in what he hoped was a soothing voice. "I won't hurt you. But your leg.... Let me call an ambu-lance for you. Or take you to the hospital."

"Please. Don't give me to snorkel. Just... just kill me."

Snorkel? What the hell did that mean? He had an accent—something Scandinavian, Tobias guessed—so maybe Tobias had misunderstood. He'd definitely understood the killing part, however, and he shook his head. The poor man must either be really wasted or having a mental health crisis.

Either way, Tobias was even more hesitant to call the cops. The local police weren't known for their sensitive handling of drug abusers or the mentally ill.

"You're going to be okay," Tobias said. "But you've hurt your leg. Can I help you?"

The man blinked at him a few times, glanced at his leg, and then shook his head miserably. "Leave me be, troll." And then he collapsed, apparently unconscious.

It was only then that Tobias noticed what the man was wearing.

CHAPTER

THREE

Tobias had been taunted with a lot worse than *troll* before, so the name-calling didn't bother him. The bleeding, previously raving man who was now out cold on his living room floor was an issue, however. After staring at him for a few more moments, Tobias worked up enough bravery to roll him onto his back and get a closer look.

It was hard to tell for sure, but Tobias thought that the bleeding was slowing down. He didn't see any other obvious wounds.

The man didn't have a phone or wallet or any ID on him, so there was no way to tell who he was or where he'd come from. The most reasonable conclusion—considering the elf outfit and pointy ears—was that he'd been attending a Christmas costume party, had ingested a mind-altering substance, and had somehow made his way into Tobias's house, wounding himself in the process.

Since the poor guy was having a bad enough day already, Tobias was hesitant to get authorities involved. He sighed, carefully gathered the man into his arms, and carried him to the bedroom, where he laid him on the bed. Then Tobias fetched the first aid kit he kept in the bathroom. It was a much larger and better-equipped kit than he'd ever thought he'd need, but Aunt Virginia used to remind him in her letters that one never knew when an emergency might arise, and even the boldest adventurer ought to be equipped for such eventualities. So far, he'd never used it for much except a skinned knee (slipped while jogging), a scorched hand (absently grabbed a hot pan handle), and a nasty splinter (foolishly attempted to repair his back deck).

Next he gathered several clean towels, a plastic basin of warm water, and a bottle of unscented antibiotic soap. He arranged everything neatly on the dresser and nightstand, opened the first aid kit, and... hesitated. Maybe he should call 911 after all.

But then the man's eyes fluttered open. He startled, moaned in pain, and went limp, his expression showing defeat.

"I'm, uh, going to take a look at your leg, okay? I've got bandages and stuff. Oh, and my name's Tobias, by the way. What's yours?"

The man's jaw worked. "Your master knows who I am, troll."

"I think you have me mixed up with someone else. I've never been into the whole BDSM scene. Don't get me wrong, I'm not judging people who enjoy it, but I don't—" He snapped his mouth shut to stop himself from babbling. Then he cleared his throat. "I don't know your name. Could you share?"

After a brief pause, the man lifted his chin. "I am Alfred Clausen, second son of Claus Clausen, and snorkel and the whole lot of you can go to Hel."

Tobias decided to concentrate on the part of this that made sense. "Nice to meet you, Alfred. Can I, uh, take a look at your leg? I'm not a doctor or a nurse or anything, by the way, but I did earn a merit badge in first aid."

Alfred turned his head and glared at the wall. "Do what you will."

Deciding that was the closest he was going to get to permission, Tobias grabbed a small pair of scissors from the kit. This made Alfred flinch, but he relaxed a little as Tobias very gingerly cut the stocking away from the wound. Tobias was proud of himself for not fainting or barfing, even when he saw that there was a long, ugly gash across Alfred's thigh. It looked as though someone had tried to saw off his leg with a bread knife, but at least the bleeding had stopped.

"You should go to the emergency room."

Alfred didn't respond.

Fine. Since he didn't appear at risk of exsanguinating, Tobias would patch him up and send him on his way. "Is there someone I can call? Someone who can come and get you?"

Alfred replied in a whisper. "Must you taunt me? Your cruelty knows no bounds."

"I'm not taunting. Seriously, just give me a phone number."

"Is snorkel hiding somewhere, laughing? He can at least show his cursed face."

So Snorkel was someone's name? "There's nobody here but me."

Alfred went silent again, so Tobias shrugged and started working on his leg. He dabbed away the dried blood with a damp towel, gently cleaned the skin with the soap, applied some antibiotic ointment to the general area, and wrapped the entire thigh in bandages. Alfred whimpered once or twice but otherwise didn't react.

The wound itself tended to, as well as Tobias was able, he considered what to do next. "Um, is it okay if I get rid of the rest of your costume? It's kind of a mess." Both the stockings and the tunic were coated in drying blood. "I'll find you something clean to wear instead."

No answer. After another shrug and more help from the scissors, Tobias managed to peel away what was left of the stockings. Alfred wasn't wearing any underwear, but it struck Tobias as even stranger that he hadn't been wearing shoes. And yet the feet of the stockings weren't dirty, so Alfred couldn't have been walking around outside like that. Another mystery.

The little scissors from the first aid kit failed the challenge of cutting the tunic fabric, so Tobias fetched a bigger pair from the kitchen junk drawer. Again,

Alfred didn't react when Tobias removed the remainder of his clothing.

Tobias reacted, however, with a shudder, because Alfred's torso was covered in vivid mottled bruises. "I don't see any more open wounds, but you could have internal injuries."

"I'm sure you'd enjoy that."

"Why would you think that? I'm *helping* you, in case you haven't noticed."

Alfred turned his head to look at Tobias through narrowed eyes. He was clearly trying to look fierce, although that was pretty ineffective considering he was naked, injured, and splayed on Tobias's galaxy-print duvet. "Why is a troll playing healer? What devilry are you plotting now?"

"I wish you'd stop calling me a troll. I told you—my name is Tobias."

"Why do you deny your nature? Do you think you are fooling me somehow? I know that you are a troll and that you will soon deliver me to Snorkel, and then all will be lost."

Maybe Alfred had suffered a head injury. Tobias tried to be patient in his response. "I don't know anyone named Snorkel. But those bruises look pretty bad. And...." He stopped and stared at Alfred's chest, because in addition to the reddish-purple splotches, there were also several tattoos of intricate abstract designs. And the tattoos were *moving*: spinning, undulating, and swaying, while also glittering as if they contained miniature disco lights.

"Um," said Tobias.

Not even glancing down to see the spectacle on his own body, Alfred continued to glare.

Tobias blinked, but nothing changed. "Um... what are those?" Living in Portland, he saw a lot of artistic tattoos, but never anything like this.

"Don't pretend more stupidity than you already possess," Alfred snarled. "Even a troll is capable of recognizing clan marks."

"Hey!" Tobias didn't offend easily, but he'd had just about enough of Alfred's gibes. He knew he should give the guy a pass due to his unsettled state of mind, except Alfred's gaze seemed clear and entirely lucid.

They stared at each other for a while, unease growing in Tobias's gut. Something here wasn't... right —aside from finding a rude, injured stranger in his living room. The weird tattoos. The costume. The delicately beautiful face, which seemed somehow familiar. The pointed ears—that flushed to their tips when Alfred was angry.

Tobias really was feeling like a dumb troll now. He just didn't understand.

Alfred must have been processing some thoughts as well, because he blinked a few times, surveyed the room, and looked back at Tobias with wide eyes. "You're not a troll."

"Thanks?"

"Are you... *human*?" He said this as if it were the most unlikely thing in the world.

Well, the second most. The *very* most unlikely thing in the world was that Alfred was an elf.

Tobias gave a distressed moan and rushed into the living room. The blood had dried on the floor; the windows and doors remained securely locked. And the doll that Aunt Virginia had given him was gone.

He made a frenzied search of the living room, finding the shoebox that now contained just the fabric and note. There was nothing under the couch cushions or under the couch itself. Nothing hidden in a corner. Certainly not behind the bookshelf, which had been firmly attached to the wall since the bungalow was built in 1927.

No. No. Absolutely *not*. It was impossible.

When Tobias shuffled hesitantly back into the bedroom, Alfred hadn't moved, but he looked as shell-shocked as Tobias felt.

"What's going on?" Tobias didn't like how wavery his own voice sounded.

"I've no idea. Please, tell me...." Alfred swallowed and didn't seem able to continue. He had an expressive face and would probably make a terrible poker player.

Tobias decided to ask one of the most bizarre questions of his life. "Are you, um, human?"

"Of course not."

Okay. Right. Of course. "Then what are you?"

"I am an elf," was the whispered reply.

There was an upholstered chair in the corner of the bedroom. As usual, it was piled with clean clothes that Tobias hadn't yet managed to fold and put away. He swept them unceremoniously to the floor and collapsed heavily onto the cushions. "I see two possibilities here. One is that you are mentally ill and/or on drugs, and after getting hurt you somehow got into my house—while wearing an elf costume and without shoes—without actually breaking in, and there's a fancy new style of tattoos I've never seen before, and you have pointy ears due to a genetic quirk or body modification surgery."

"That's not—"

"But I was taught that Occam's Razor is generally a good guide."

Alfred shook his head. "I do not know him."

"It's a heuristic, not a person. It says that when there are competing hypotheses, the simplest one is usually more accurate."

"I see." Alfred furrowed his brow. "And what are your competing hypotheses now?"

"I already told you one. It's pretty complex. The other possibility is that the elf doll Aunt Virginia gave me has somehow come alive."

That didn't sound any more plausible out loud than it did in his head, but then, the complex possibility made no sense at all.

"Doll?" whispered Alfred.

Might as well spit it out. "My aunt gave me an elf doll. I think it used to belong to her wizard husband. I put it on my shelf yesterday, and now here you are, and it's gone, and you look exactly like it did, including even a hurt leg, and Jesus this is insane but I honestly think it's true and I've never heard of anything like this and I don't know what to do!"

That was more like barfing than spitting it out, and Tobias had to pause to catch his breath.

Alfred, meanwhile, had gone incredibly pale. He worked his mouth as if he were trying to say something but couldn't find the words, then let out a gasping sort of sigh.

"I've been transferred," he said.

And fainted dead away.

CHAPTER

FOUR

"This is very good tea." Alfred attempted a smile.

Tobias had propped him up using several pillows, and Alfred was able to hold the cup himself, although his hands trembled. At least he'd regained some color in his cheeks, and now that Tobias had tucked a blanket around him, his bruises and bandaged leg weren't visible.

"It's my favorite oolong." Tobias had brewed a mug for himself too, hoping the familiar beverage would steady him. It had achieved only limited success, and his mind still felt like that trippy tunnel scene in the old Willy Wonka movie.

"I am sorry I called you a troll. I was terribly rude. It's only... you're very large and so are trolls, and I assumed.... Well, I apologize."

Tobias had long since gotten over feeling offended; he had bigger fish to fry. Like the fact that there was an elf in his bed. He was finding it surprisingly easy to accept the situation, maybe because it was better to believe in elves than to fear the loss of his sanity. He smiled at Alfred. "So trolls are real. The under-the-bridges trolls. Not the obnoxious online trolls; I know *they* exist."

"I'm not sure what you're talking about, but yes, trolls are real. They're dangerous, and many of them are in Snorkel's employment." Alfred shook his head slightly. "I should have known better. You're much more handsome than a troll."

Feeling his cheeks heat, Tobias tried to stay focused. "Who's Snorkel?"

"It's Snjokarl. S-n-j-o-k-a-r-l. And he's...." Alfred shuddered so violently that Tobias thought he'd spill his tea.

"Hang on. You're still pretty banged up and I think you've had a major shock. Hell, we both have. How about if I get you something to eat and then you take a nap? We can talk later."

"You're very kind. Thank you."

The blush intensified. "Okay, what do you want—"

"Wait. Please, am I safe here?"

"I'm not going to let anyone harm you." Tobias was surprised by the intensity and truth of this statement.

Looking slightly relieved, Alfred set his free hand on Tobias's knee. "But are *you* safe, my friend?"

A serious question called for a serious answer, no matter how distracting that hand was. "I'm clearly clueless about whatever's going on with you and probably about a whole lot of other stuff too. But this is my home, so it's as safe as any place can be, and I'll do my best to keep it that way."

Although Alfred still looked troubled, he nodded.

After a quick consultation regarding elven dietary preferences—it turned out that Alfred wasn't picky—Tobias cooked a nice grilled cheese sandwich and heated some tomato soup. But when he carried them into the bedroom, Alfred was already fast asleep, and Tobias didn't have the heart to wake him. He ate the food himself, figuring he could make more when his guest woke up.

Afterward, a bit at loose ends, Tobias scrubbed the blood off his living room floor and threw away the scraps of Alfred's clothing. He examined the shoebox from Aunt Virginia, but although he'd kept the fabric and note, they didn't provide any hints about what to do with Alfred. He now understood the note in a very different way than on his initial reading, however. Olve Lange hadn't been worried about a damaged Christmas decoration; he'd been concerned about a living elf.

And now Tobias was too.

Eventually he sat in his bedroom armchair, playing on his phone. He must have dozed off, though, because he was startled awake by a crash and a yelp of pain. He found Alfred curled up on the floor, moaning over his leg.

"What are you doing? You're hurt!" Tobias lifted him back onto the bed. It was the second time he'd had

Alfred in his arms, only this time Alfred was conscious and naked, which made it quite a different experience. Probably for both of them.

Any naughty thoughts were sidetracked, however, when Tobias spied the blood seeping through the bandages. "Oh no," he moaned. "You need to see a doctor and get that cared for properly."

"I thought you were a healer."

"I'm a data engineer."

That got him a blank look. Then he dithered, because although Alfred certainly needed stitches at the very least—and possibly a lot more—Tobias wasn't sure how the emergency room staff would react to treating an elf.

Alfred sighed. "I'll be all right eventually. Have you a needle and thread?"

"You're not planning to sew it up yourself!"

"I was rather hoping you would."

Tobias *did* know how to sew, in fact. He'd taken classes a few years earlier because he couldn't find shirts he liked in his size. He had actually become pretty good at it, and he had a sewing machine in the bedroom closet. But sewing clothes was a lot different than sewing… flesh. He shuddered.

"I'll do it if you're unable," Alfred said quietly. "And don't worry. My injuries aren't mortal and I heal quickly."

"Hang on."

Tobias hurried to the kitchen, where he quickly fried up another sandwich and reheated the rest of the soup. While Alfred ate, Tobias dug into his sewing basket. He wasted a minute or two trying to decide on a thread color before remembering that the first aid kit had suturing supplies—no doubt a better choice than fuchsia-colored cotton. Next he watched a YouTube video on technique. It didn't look too difficult, but then again, the person in the video was probably well trained.

"That was an excellent meal." Alfred wiped his mouth with a paper napkin. "And this bed is very large and comfortable. You're being very kind to me."

"Let's see if you still think so after I stab you with this." Tobias held up the sterile needle.

"I believe I could withstand many tortures if they came from your hands."

Was that *flirting*? Tobias was bad at recognizing that kind of thing when it came from regular people; he wasn't at all equipped to identify an elf's intentions. He shot Alfred a wan smile, sat on the mattress, and carefully unwrapped the bandages.

Alfred seemed oblivious to his own nudity. That was not true for Tobias, especially as he was tending to Alfred's upper thigh, but at least it slightly distracted him from the blood. And from the full realization that it was a living body he was sewing and not fabric.

"I'm worried about infection," he said after he completed the first stitch. "I've done what I can to avoid it, but—"

"It's not a concern for me."

"Do you mean you're not worried about it, or you don't get infections?"

Alfred shrugged—and winced, likely due to the bruising. "I heal quickly and I don't get ill easily."

"How did this happen to you?"

"Snjokarl."

"I still don't know who that is."

"Consider yourself fortunate." Alfred closed his eyes for a minute. He was clearly being stoic about the sewing, which had to hurt. Hell, his entire body must be hurting. But evidently this Snjokarl guy was a bigger deal than the pain.

When Alfred opened his eyes again, he gave Tobias a weak smile. "I owe you an explanation, at least, in return for your hospitality. How much would you like to know?"

Curiosity had always been one of Tobias's weaknesses. "Everything." Before Alfred could speak, though, Tobias shook his head. "But you've had a hell of a day. Honestly, so have I. Maybe you should just take it easy and tell me tomorrow."

"I may... I may stay here?"

"Of course. Unless there's somewhere else you'd rather be."

"I don't...." Alfred chewed on his lip and looked so woeful that Tobias would have hugged him if he hadn't been sewing up his leg. "I've never been here before. I don't know anyone, or—"

"You know me."

Tobias surprised even himself with that statement.

Not because he regretted it—he most certainly didn't —but because he was so sure it was the right thing to say. Usually he stumbled over words when talking with other people, but not now. And when Alfred gave him the sweetest, softest smile, Tobias blushed and firmly returned his attention to the stitching. But his insides felt as warm and gooey as if he were a fresh cinnamon roll, and that wasn't a bad thing at all.

"I am so sorry I was rude to you," Alfred said after a moment.

"You weren't. You were afraid, and who could blame you?"

"I was rude. I can be a bit... imperious, I'm afraid. My father is a king, you see, and— Was. He *was* a king. Now I suppose my brother is king instead."

This was clearly a fraught topic, which Alfred definitely didn't need right now, so Tobias tried to steer the conversation in another direction. "How should I address you? I've never met a prince before. Just a countess."

To Tobias's considerable relief, Alfred managed a small chuckle. "Under the circumstances, you may address me however you wish. But I think I'd most prefer Alfie. It's what my friends call me."

Yep, definitely a cinnamon roll. Tobias managed a nod before concentrating on the final two stitches.

By the time he finished and cleaned everything up, the wound looked a bit better but Alfie's face was drawn with pain and exhaustion. Tobias brought him more soup, this time chicken noodle, and more tea.

Once that was consumed, he helped him lie flat again and tucked him back in, noting that the bedding should be changed as soon as Alfie had recovered a little. Alfie fell asleep almost at once.

Tobias spent time puttering around: cleaning the kitchen, checking his email, rereading the note from Olve Lange. Then it occurred to him that Aunt Virginia might be able to shed some light on the situation. Although he had her number, he'd never spoken to her by phone. Apparently she'd long ago heard her voice on someone else's answering machine and, appalled at how she sounded, thereafter refused to talk on the phone unless absolutely necessary. So he wasn't surprised when she didn't answer, and there was no way for him to leave a message.

Since Aunt Virginia was a dead end, Tobias turned to the internet. It was about as helpful as he expected, which was to say not at all. He found lots of stories and memes about elves of several varieties—especially those related to Christmas, Tolkien, and Nordic/Germanic folklore—but although it was interesting, he doubted that much of it pertained to his current guest. A side quest regarding trolls was similarly useless, and all the search for Snjokarl taught him was that *snjókarl* was Icelandic for *snowman*. Whoever Alfie was so scared of, Alfie doubted it was Olaf from Disney's *Frozen*.

The internet was also useless on the subject of dolls being turned into living beings or vice versa, although he got a lot of hits for the Chucky and Barbie movie franchises.

After a long sit on the couch with his laptop, Tobias had just stood for a stretch when he heard a rustling from the bedroom. He hurried in and discovered Alfie sitting on the edge of the bed, face contorted in pain.

"Hey! You're going to fall again."

"But my bladder is going to burst and I don't wish to soil your bed."

"I don't think you should walk on that leg."

Tobias thought quickly, trotted into the kitchen, and returned with an empty mayo jar he hadn't yet taken out to the recycling bin. He handed it to Alfie with a little flourish, then politely turned his back while Alfie used it. After he emptied it into the toilet and washed his hands, he returned to help Alfie back into bed.

"I feel so useless," Alfie moaned.

"You're hurt. Give yourself a break."

"I'll bet that if *you* were in my shoes, you would still be capable of caring for yourself. You're strong as a *snjómaður*."

Although Tobias was pleased at what he took to be a compliment, he frowned. "Is that the same as Snjokarl?"

Alfie looked horrified. "Gods no! A snjómaður is a very large being with thick white fur. They're exceedingly powerful. But they're also quite gentle unless provoked. They prefer solitude most of the time, but

I'm acquainted with a few of them who don't mind sharing some mead now and then."

Oh. So yetis were real too. Tobias wondered what other mythical creatures weren't so mythical after all.

"I'm a big baby about pain," he said. "When I was twelve, I fell off my skateboard and broke my arm, and I guarantee I wasn't the least bit stoic about it. I lolled on the couch for days as if I'd been mortally wounded."

A smile teased at the corners of Alfie's mouth. "But you were a child."

"I wasn't that young. My poor mom was busy enough already without having to wait on me."

"Your father couldn't help?"

Tobias shrugged. "Never had one. Hang on." He went into the living room and returned with a framed photo from the bookshelf, which he handed to Alfie, who examined it closely.

His mother was in a pretty green dress and, since the photo had been taken at Tobias's college graduation, he wore a cap and gown. The two of them looked like complete opposites. He was tall, bulky, and pale, while she was tiny and had dark brown skin.

Alfie, unlike most people, didn't remark on their physical dissimilarity. "I can see in her eyes how much she loves you."

"She did. She died not long after this photo was taken."

Alfie looked stricken. "I am so sorry."

"I still miss her. She adopted me when I was an infant and she was a single woman in her late forties.

Some people thought that was a bad idea, but I couldn't have hoped for a better mother. She was brilliant—a university professor—and strong and supportive and kind."

"Ah," said Alfie as he handed back the photo. "Then I am grateful to her for teaching you so well."

The cinnamon roll feeling was back.

Tobias busied himself for a bit, checking Alfie's wounds—which looked no worse, at least—and fussing with the blankets and pillows. He brought him tea and water and, when Alfie admitted that he could eat, a bowl of pasta with marinara sauce. He also brought in a comb for his thick blond hair and a damp washcloth and plastic basin of warm water so he could freshen up a little. By the time Alfie had peed again, the pain lines had returned to his face.

"Get a good night's sleep," Tobias instructed him. "That always helps."

"Is this *your* bed?" Alfie looked troubled.

"Yes."

"Then where will you sleep?"

Tobias had been considering that very question. His spare bedroom was set up as an office and had no bed. He'd once owned an inflatable mattress he'd bought for camping trips, but it had proved too flimsy for his body, and if he still owned it, he didn't know where it was or whether it was still usable. The floor would kill his back. That left the couch, which was oversize but still not really big enough for him. He'd napped on it before, though, so he guessed he could manage even if he'd be scrunched up for a night.

"I'll be just in the next room. Call if you need anything."

"I can't take your bed!"

Alfie moved as if he were going to sit up, so Tobias gently pushed him back down. "I don't want to have to sew you up again. Do me a favor and stay here, okay?"

"It's a large bed. There's room enough for us both."

That was technically true. But between Alfie's injuries and his nudity, Tobias deemed it best to sleep somewhere else. His life was not a romance trope. "I snore. Now get some sleep. I want you in good enough shape to share your backstory tomorrow."

Reluctantly, Alfie nodded. Tobias rearranged the pillows and turned out the lights. "I'll leave the door open a crack if that's okay. So I can hear you better if you need anything." Or if he collapsed onto the floor again.

As Tobias was easing the door closed, Alfie's quiet voice came out of the darkness. "Thank you, my friend. Your mother would be so proud of you."

FIVE

S o it had not been just a very weird dream. When Tobias woke up in the morning, muscles stiff and joints crackly from sleeping on the couch, there was still an elf in his bed.

He couldn't tell whether Alfie looked improved over the previous day, but he wasn't bleeding and didn't look worse, so Tobias counted it as a win. Alfie greeted him with a warm smile. "I must be keeping you from your regular life."

"My work can wait." That was true, although Tobias rarely acknowledged it, even to himself. None of his clients were particularly desperate to get anything from him at the moment, with the holidays upon them and lots of people on vacation. But when he kept his head buried in the job, he felt important and didn't notice his loneliness as much. Today, however, he could accomplish those goals without his computer's help.

"Do you, uh, need to use the mayo jar?"

Alfie glanced at the side table, where the item in question waited. "I was hoping perhaps I might be able to make it to the toilet this morning, with a bit of help."

Although Tobias wasn't sure that was wise, he understood Alfie's desire to hang on to some dignity, so he nodded. "We can give it a try."

Alfie managed to sit up with help and then twisted so his feet were on the floor. His face was tight with pain, but he gripped Tobias's arm and slowly stood. "I'm normally very graceful," he said through gritted teeth. "I've won ribbons for my dancing."

"The last time I tried was in junior high when we had to do square dancing. I was awful. Stomped all over everyone's feet, messed up the steps, couldn't keep to the beat to save my life." It had been acutely embarrassing, but then so was virtually everything else at that age. He'd tried hard to remain in the background of things, hoping nobody would notice him, but that became increasingly difficult once his growth spurt hit and he went from large to massive.

"I could teach you how, once I've recovered."

Tobias thought about what private lessons might entail—lots of touching and attention to his physical self—and felt a rush of desire so strong that his knees felt weak. He had to remind himself that he was supposed to be supporting Alfie, not lusting after him.

"I'm probably a hopeless case."

"No, I could teach you," Alfie repeated confidently.

It took a long time to cross the room, walk the few

steps down the hall, and enter the bathroom, and Tobias ended up bearing a good portion of Alfie's weight. For once he was happy about his size and strength because they allowed him to help.

Alfie didn't let go until he was seated on the toilet. "Thank you, Tobias."

"I'll give you some privacy. Call when you're ready to walk back. Don't try it by yourself."

"You're quite good at looking stern." Alfie didn't quite smile, but humor definitely danced in those blue eyes.

Tobias lurked in the hallway, marveling at the sudden strange turn in his life.

Alfie needed even more support on the way back, and both he and Tobias were relieved once he was tucked back into bed. "Do you have bathrooms where you come from?" asked Tobias while adjusting the pillow.

"Of course. We're not barbarians."

"I just thought... I don't know. I didn't picture elves with modern plumbing, I guess." Somehow the folklore never seemed to mention elfin toilets.

"My chambers at the palace have a water closet with a toilet and bidet, as well as a bath room with a tub large enough to invite two or three friends to join me." He waggled his eyebrows suggestively, but then his face fell. "Had. I'll never see the palace again."

"Why not?"

Alfie spread his arms. "I'm here. I have no means to return to my world."

"Your *world*? Wait. Let me go make some breakfast and then maybe you can explain a little."

While Alfie dozed, Tobias hurried through morning ablutions, threw on some clean clothes, and prepared bacon, pancakes, and tea. He sat in the bedroom chair to eat while Alfie tackled his meal with enthusiasm. When Tobias offered to change the bedding, which harbored crumbs and a little dried blood, Alfie shook his head. "It can wait. You asked about my world."

Ah. It was finally story time. "Is it really a whole separate world? Like a different planet or something?" Maybe elves were aliens.

"It's more like... a different layer. Imagine two pieces of cloth, one floating on top of the other. They have much in common, but each is independent and self-contained. A bit of space separates them, and generally there is no interaction between them. But at certain times, one of the pieces curves so as to touch the other. This never lasts long, but while it does, those who exist on one piece can view those on the other." He paused and cocked his head, clearly waiting to see whether Tobias understood.

Surprisingly, Tobias did. In fact, he remembered something Aunt Virginia had told him. *The border between the possible and the impossible becomes more permeable.* "Is later December one of those times?"

Pleased, Alfie flashed him a grin. "Yes! During the winter and summer solstices, our worlds can reliably be expected to touch. It's less predictable at other times of the year, and sometimes it's a particular event in one world or the other that causes the warping of the fabric."

"So when this happens, you guys can see what we're up to."

"To a limited extent." Alfie shrugged. "We see enough to have some notion of events in your world. And sometimes your people catch glimpses of us."

Realization hit. "That's why we have stories about Christmas elves, isn't it?"

"I believe so. Your people have other lore that we've inspired as well, about brownies, goblins, pixies, and boggarts."

Although all of this should have seemed like a load of nonsense straight out of a novel, Tobias had no trouble believing it. After all, he had an elf in his bed. Besides, the explanation made sense, like a math problem where both sides of the equation equaled out.

"How long does this, um, warping last? Do we still have time to get you back home?"

Alfie bowed his head and gave it a small shake. "I haven't explained properly. We can see the other world, but we can't move between them."

"But—"

Alfie held up a hand. "I know. I'm here. What I mean is that very few of us can make this transfer. Powerful wizards are capable of it, and some of them can even transfer others. I imagine that's what happened to me, although I don't know why. Also, there are some beings who can sometimes do this.

Trolls, for instance. Nixies. Selkies, grims, and the hafg-ufa." He sighed. "Not humans, and not elves."

Now Tobias had a better understanding of why Alfie had been so upset when he learned where he was. Ready to comfort him, Tobias had a rather shocking thought and he cleared his throat. "You know how I told you that, um, my aunt gave me a doll that turned into, well, you?"

"Of course."

"Her second husband was a wizard and the doll, uh, well, *you*—dammit, this is awkward!—belonged to him."

"That makes sense. He's likely the one who trans-ferred me." Alfie sighed. "And you're using the past tense, so I assume he's deceased."

Tobias shuffled his feet like a nervous schoolboy. "Um, yeah. Or disappeared maybe? And the thing is, he's been gone for... a while. Before I was born. So it's been a long time since you were transferred."

To Tobias's surprise, Alfie gave him a small smile. "You're concerned for me. Thank you. But the temporal issue isn't a worry. If I could somehow return, I would find myself at more or less the same place whence I left, and likely not more than a year or so later. Which would be problematic, actually, because I was very nearly killed. I'm guessing that your wizard's interven-tion saved my life."

That made Tobias blink a few times as the gears turned slowly in his head. "So you were injured *before* Aunt Virginia's husband magicked you." That was a relief. Not that he'd ever believe she was married to a villain, but the wizard could have accidentally hurt Alfie. It sounded, however, as if he had been trying to protect him. "But all those years when you were a doll, you must have been…. I can't even imagine how awful."

Another smile. "I wasn't aware, Tobias. I didn't suffer."

That mattered to Tobias. Not that he generally enjoyed other people's misery, but he found himself especially distressed by the idea of Alfie's. Although Tobias hadn't asked for the responsibility of caring for an elf, he took it seriously. And besides, he liked Alfie, who was doing his best under what must be devastating circumstances, and who was… nice.

Tobias wanted to know a lot more about how Alfie got hurt, who that Snjokarl guy was, and how Aunt Virginia's husband had become involved. But there were more important things than simply satisfying his curiosity.

"You're looking a little more chipper," he said. "Do you want to get dressed?"

"Does my nudity *bother* you?" Alfie stressed the word and, in case Tobias hadn't caught his meaning, waggled his eyebrows.

Although Tobias blushed, for once he didn't stumble over his words. "Not bothered at all, but since you're not in any condition for either of us to enjoy it properly…." Oh my God, he was flirting. With an elf.

And the elf was laughing, seemingly delighted.

"How am I so fortunate to have acquired a savior who is handsome, strong, kind, *and* amusing?"

Tobias's blush intensified.

With some difficulty, he found a pair of navy-colored sweatpants that would probably work, at least for the time being. Alfie could tighten the drawstring waist, and the elastic bands around the ankles would keep the hems from dragging. He also gave him his favorite T-shirt, made of incredibly silky cotton the color of ripe plums. Alfie needed help putting it all on, but together they managed and then followed up with another bathroom trip. This time Alfie didn't lean so heavily on Tobias.

Alfie brought them to a halt as they were returning to the bedroom. "May I perhaps spend some time out of bed?"

"Are you sure you're up to it?"

"Lying around will do nothing but make me wallow in self-pity."

It would also be easier to change the bedding, so Tobias led him into the living room and quickly dragged the sheet and blanket off the couch so Alfie could sit.

"Is *this* what I consigned you to by commandeering your bed?"

Tobias shrugged. "It's a couch, not a torture chamber. It's pretty comfy, actually."

"For sitting, perhaps. But it's far too small for a man of your impressive stature. You must have been miserable."

Actually, Tobias hadn't slept well at all, but he wasn't about to admit it. He had just opened his mouth to change the subject when there was a heavy knock on the door. Crap. It was possibly religious recruiters or a salesperson, or even more likely, his slightly off neighbor who liked to complain about the trees growing in front of Tobias's house: three impressively large Douglas-firs. Tobias liked them because they were pretty and attracted birds, but the weirdo neighbor was convinced they were going to fall any minute and take out the whole block. He got especially nervous when the weather turned icy.

"Hang on." Tobias strode to the door.

It wasn't the neighbor. It was two men who didn't look much like Jehovah's Witnesses or solar panel salesmen. They were as tall as Tobias and as heavily built, with bushy blond hair and even bushier blond beards. Their clothing—tall black boots, dun-colored baggy hose, and taupe tunics—made them look like escapees from a Renaissance faire. Tobias noted the leather belts with knife sheaths at both hips.

The men looked surprised to see Tobias. "You have him already?" one of them growled. "Why didn't you say something?"

"I think you have the wrong address."

Tobias started to close the door, but they pushed past him and lunged straight at Alfie, who cried out in distress.

"Tobias, run!" he shouted as he tried to scramble away. But his leg was unsteady and the two men were on him at once, one of them slugging him in the belly while the other tried to wrestle him into a rough bear hug. Despite his injuries and the gut punch, Alfie put up a fight, squirming, kicking, and biting like an angry bobcat. He might have made some headway had he faced only one large assailant, but couldn't manage two.

Just inside the front door was a small wooden table, on top of which sat a heavy marble statue of two naked Greeks wrestling. Without pausing to consider whether it was a good idea, Tobias picked up the statue, rushed a few steps closer to the melee, and threw it with all his strength at the nearer stranger's head.

The man dropped to the floor with a solid thud.

Before Tobias could celebrate his success, the second man roared, let go of Alfie, and tackled Tobias.

The last time Tobias had been in a fight was in second grade, when a classmate named Logan Dankworth had teased him about not having a father. Both boys had ended up crying, Tobias had been sent to the principal's office, and his mother had given him a long talk about avoiding violence unless absolutely necessary. None of that had prepared him to go hand-to-hand with an enraged giant.

But Tobias was equally as big, and his adrenaline was flowing. After a lifetime of holding himself back and trying to remain unthreatening and unobtrusive, it felt *amazing* to just... let go. If Alfie had been an angry bobcat, Tobias was a furious grizzly. He roared and squeezed and hit, and although the other guy was whaling on him too, Tobias didn't feel any pain. In fact, as the two of them rolled around on the floor, Tobias almost wanted to laugh with the joy of battle.

And then something went *thunk* and his opponent slumped in his grip.

Tobias scrambled out from under him to discover Alfie standing a few inches away, face grim, the marble wrestlers clutched in both hands.

"Run," Alfie pleaded. "Before more of them show up."

Slightly out of breath, Tobias shook his head in an attempt to clear it. "More of who?"

"Trolls, of course."

Oh. Of course. Tobias stared at the two unmoving lumps. "Are they dead?"

"I don't know and I don't particularly care. They would have taken me to Snjokarl if you hadn't saved me—and gods, *thank* you, Tobias—but there are dozens more in his employment."

Still trying to process the fact that he'd just fought a fucking troll, Tobias rubbed his head. "I should call the police." He wouldn't have to explain the troll part; he could just quite honestly say that they'd intruded into his home and attacked his guest.

"Will the police protect you when the next round of trolls appears?"

Tobias rather doubted that. He couldn't exactly

request a personal guard, and he didn't have complete confidence that the cops would be sympathetic at all. "So what should we do?"

Alfie stood silently for a moment before shuffling back to the couch and collapsing heavily onto the cushion. "Leave. Come back in a couple of days. By then I'll be in Snjokarl's hands and I doubt he'll bother sending anyone after you. You'll be safe."

"I'm not going to abandon you!" Tobias was indignant.

"Then I'll go."

Alfie started to stand, but Tobias hurried over and gently urged him back down. "Go where? I'm not going to just kick you out so you can...." Not quite willing to finish the thought, he waved a hand in the direction of the trolls.

"You've already done so much for me." Alfie's voice was gentle. "I'm not your responsibility."

This had been the most confusing two days of Tobias's life, but he was dead sure of one thing. He bent so he could look Alfie straight in the eyes. "But you are. Aunt Virginia gave you to *me*, and she did it for a reason. I'm not letting either of you down."

Alfie reached up and stroked Tobias's cheek, making him shiver with pleasure. "You are magnificent," Alfie said.

Although Tobias would have very much liked to pursue that thought—and to feel that warm hand on other parts of his body—now was clearly not the time.

There were two unconscious or possibly dead trolls in his living room, with more lively ones on the way.

He straightened, put his hands on his hips, and confidently announced, "I know what we need to do."

CHAPTER

SIX

A pparently Alfie had never been in a car before, and it seemed that his pain was subdued by the novelty of zooming down I-5.

"Are you sure you're not bleeding?" Tobias asked for the third or fourth time. He didn't want to take his eyes from the road.

Alfie reached over and patted Tobias's leg. "You saved me. You're a hero."

"Pfft." Tobias didn't feel heroic. In fact, he kept remembering the noise the statue made when it hit each troll's head, and the memory made him queasy. At least he hadn't seen any blood. "Do you think they're dead?"

"Perhaps. But trolls are hard to kill. In any case, don't feel bad about it. Given the opportunity, they would have murdered you. And my fate... well, I'd prefer not to speak of it."

Tobias frowned at the traffic in front of him. "I was

always the biggest kid in my class, and because of that, Mom would tell me that I had a special duty to be careful with others. She said I should never let my temper cause me to harm anyone."

"But surely she wouldn't have disapproved of protecting yourself—or a wounded charge—from two vicious attackers."

"I guess not." Tobias sighed and frowned even more fiercely. "But the thing is... I *liked* it. The fighting part, I mean." That was hard to admit, especially to himself.

For a mile or two, Alfie was silent, and if not for his warm hand still resting on Tobias's leg, Tobias might have assumed he was shocked or upset. When Alfie spoke, however, his voice was gentle. "I don't believe anyone can be blamed for how they feel—only for the actions they take. And I don't believe you've abused your strength or allowed bloodlust to rule you."

Bloodlust. Tobias shuddered.

Alfie's comments had made him feel slightly better, though, and he shot him a grateful smile. The smile turned into a semi-hysterical guffaw when Tobias realized they were driving past the Enchanted Forest theme park. He'd adored that place when he was a boy —little knowing that one day he'd meet fairy tale beings in the real world.

"It's a pretty long drive to San Francisco," he said after a while. "Ten hours or more. Would we be safe if we took two days to do it? If the trolls won't track us down, we could stay the night in a hotel somewhere."

He could have managed the uninterrupted drive but was concerned about Alfie, still recovering from injuries.

"I think that should be fine."

Although Tobias would have preferred something more reassuring than *I think*, he'd take what he could get. "Get some rest, then. I'll stop for food and gas in a couple of hours." When Alfie made a grunt that may have been agreement, Tobias added, "You can recline your seat if you want. There's a handle on—"

"I'm comfortable, thank you." Instead of sleeping, Alfie seemed intent on watching the scenery. Trees, fields, occasional small cities: maybe those looked exotic to him.

Tobias had so many questions that he didn't know where to begin, but he also didn't want to disturb Alfie's peace. The poor guy had been through a lot in a short time. So instead, Tobias ruminated on the events back in Portland. After the troll attack, he'd hurriedly gathered his laptop, some clothes for both of them, and a few other belongings. Then he'd followed Alfie's directions and dragged the trolls into the narrow space between his house and the neighbor's fence. At the time, Tobias had thought that the trolls were still breathing, but he wasn't sure and he didn't waste time finding out. Then he'd helped Alfie into the car and headed south.

If the trolls were dead, someone would notice eventually. They wouldn't be visible from the street due to some shrubbery, and decomposition might take some time in the chilly air. But they were big, and a pair of big corpses would make themselves known. Then, presumably, the police would be called, and Tobias would have some difficult explanations ahead of him when he returned.

He decided not to think about that.

The better option was that the trolls would wake up—maybe they already had—and get the hell out of there. Which would be nice from a not-going-to-jail perspective but would also mean they'd be back, probably soon, with reinforcements. And while Alfie might be their target, they probably held a pretty dim view of Tobias at this point.

Life had been a lot simpler before Aunt Virginia gave him that box. With Alfie beside him, however, bright and beautiful and very much alive, Tobias held few regrets.

"That was an interesting weapon," Alfie said out of the blue, somewhere south of Eugene.

"What?"

"The one you chose to fight the trolls."

"It's just, um, art. And it was handy."

"Yes. But presumably you didn't acquire it with the intention of using it to brain assailants."

"Presumably," Tobias muttered. Then, because Alfie was waiting patiently, he sighed and explained. "It was a gift from Aunt Virginia, actually. When I was a freshman in college, I complained to my mom about having to study the ancient Greeks. I didn't think they were particularly relevant to me. I guess Mom told

Aunt Virginia, and my aunt sent me the statue because the wrestlers are hot and she figured I'd suddenly find the Greeks way more interesting."

Alfie chuckled softly. "And was she right?"

"I didn't become a classical scholar or anything, but... yeah. I passed the class."

"So the statue has been useful more than once. Your aunt must care about you very much."

"She and Mom are the only people who ever—" Tobias stopped, not wanting to sound too pathetic. But there was Alfie's hand on Tobias's leg again, and somehow confessions seemed to flow when he was around. "Who ever loved me," he finished quietly.

"Now I love you as well."

Tobias nearly drove off the road. "We just met!" he protested after he'd steered the car back to safety.

"And in that short time, you have proved kind, considerate, and brave. You have given up your bed, cared for me tenderly and with respect for my dignity, defended me physically, and fled your home at a moment's notice in order to help me. I've never met anyone like you. And don't discount my love, please. An elfin prince does not easily or capriciously allow himself to love."

Since Tobias couldn't come up with a reasonable response, he remained silent. But—despite his bizarre and precarious circumstances—some of the jagged places of his soul felt soothed.

THEY MADE a pit stop in Roseburg and, after enjoying a fried chicken sandwich, Alfie fell asleep. That left Tobias alone with his thoughts, a solitude that he found surprisingly uncomfortable despite being how he'd spent most of his life. He turned the radio on low and found a classic rock station that reminded him of his mother, who used to belt out Grateful Dead and AC/DC songs on their road trips together.

Alfie stirred a little south of the California border. He groaned a bit as he moved but quickly went silent and patted Tobias's arm. "I'm sorry I'm such poor company."

"You need your rest."

"Even so."

"I'm going to stop for the night sometime soon." They were at about the halfway point, the sun had set, and Tobias was hungry again. He was also tired of staring at the highway.

"All right." Alfie yawned and then laughed at himself. "I promise, I'm usually not this useless."

"You've, uh, had a pretty rough time of things."

"I have. I was going to tell you my tale, wasn't I? Before the trolls interrupted us. Shall I do it now?"

"Please." Tobias may have answered a bit over-enthusiastically, failing in his attempt to play it cool and pretend like he hadn't been dying to hear. But he'd been waiting for over a day now, and patience wasn't always his best virtue. Honestly, he felt as if he'd exercised admirable restraint in not pestering Alfie to spill hours ago.

As if reading Tobias's thoughts, Alfie chuckled again. It was a very sexy chuckle, the kind that sent Tobias's mind all sorts of naughty places despite his overwhelming curiosity. That laugh reminded Tobias that it had been months since he'd managed a quick hookup with anyone and much longer since he'd had sex with anyone who wasn't a stranger. Until Alfie came along, he wasn't sure of the last time he'd been touched.

"My father is—*was*, dammit—Claus Clausen, and he was our king. That sounds rather more impressive than it is. Ours is a very small kingdom and we owe our allegiance to the Emperor of the Sparkling Plains. My father was a good ruler: intelligent and just and beloved by our people. The Emperor considered him an important advisor."

Alfie's voice rang with pride, which Tobias understood. He'd felt that way about his own mother. She hadn't been royalty, of course, but she'd been brilliant and *good*. Alfie had also used the past tense.

"Has your father passed away?" Tobias asked gently.

"He... yes." A heavy sigh. "The Emperor has been losing strength. Our world is intimately connected with yours, you see, and I believe that your changing weather patterns have resulted in the waning of the Emperor's power."

"Climate change is ruining things for you too?" Tobias was appalled at the concept. It was horrifying enough to see people destroying one world, but to know that they were damaging another as well.... It was awful beyond belief.

"Yes." Alfie was clearly saddened. "And there are those who would prey upon his weakness. They would like to see the empire disintegrate so their own authority can grow. My older brother is one of them."

Tobias, who had an intuition regarding where this might be going, took his gaze off the road just long enough to glance at Alfie's bleak expression. "Oh no," Tobias said.

Alfie gave one of his comforting leg squeezes. "Kol and I have never gotten on well. He's three years older than I am and has never let me forget that he is the heir. Father tried so hard to teach Kol kindness, humility, and patience, but with little success. And I was not blameless. Free of the heir's responsibilities, I've often been a bit, well, wild. Kol envies my relative freedom."

Silence settled between them for a few minutes, the tires humming against the pavement and the engine purring along. They were surrounded by trees now, and the forest seemed especially dark and mysterious, especially since there were fewer cars about.

"Do you have siblings?" Alfie's question surprised Tobias.

"It was just Mom and me."

He had sometimes longed for a brother or sister, but single parenthood was hard enough with one child, he supposed. And a greedy part of him treasured having his mother to himself.

"I believe that family relationships tend to be

complicated under any circumstances. But when the family is royal, that can add even more layers."

Tobias thought about all the headlines and memes he'd seen about the British royals and nodded.

Alfie continued his story. "Father and Kol argued about what to do regarding the Emperor and the empire, but Kol could only press so hard. Although I backed Father, he asked me to stay quiet about it, since my open involvement in the disagreement would only make things worse. He hoped that eventually Kol would change his views."

It wasn't fair. All the Christmas season kitsch depicted elves as jolly little fellows concerned mostly with making toys and maybe baking cookies. In reality, though, it sounded as if they had much more serious problems to deal with. The lore should have acknowledged that elves' lives could also be tough.

"Kol *didn't* change his views, I take it?" Tobias prompted.

"I think he might have eventually. He's not... not evil." Alfie's voice was pained. "But he fell under Snjokarl's influence."

Tobias definitely wanted to hear more about this, but towns were few and far between in this area and they were approaching one large enough to advertise lodging. "I'm going to stop in a sec. Tell me the rest over dinner?"

"Yes, good. I need to think about how to explain this fairly."

The next exit led them through the trees. "Reminds me of home," Alfie said wistfully.

They drove down a slope, past a few blocks of houses followed by a few blocks of businesses. Beyond that was a motor court inn: about a half-dozen small cabins with a parking lot on one side and a river on the other. The neon sign glowed *Vacancy*, which was a relief.

Alfie seemed content to remain in the car while Tobias ducked into the office, where a sleepy-looking older man swiped Tobias's credit card and handed over a key to Cabin C. With Tobias steadying him, Alfie made it into the cabin and collapsed heavily onto a chair that looked too spindly to hold Tobias's bulk.

"Quaint," Tobias commented. The décor was... vintage, to put it kindly, with a cabin-in-the-woods theme to the furniture, bedding, and artwork. Definitely not luxe, but it was clean and there were no lurking trolls, which was good enough for now. There was also only one bed, but it was a king and therefore plenty big enough to share.

"Do you want me to bring us some food?"

Alfie shook his head. "Give me a few moments and then I should like to accompany you, if it isn't far."

Although Tobias was a bit doubtful about Alfie moving around too much, he didn't argue. "There's a place just down the road. Do you want me to check your wounds first?"

"No. I'm fine." Alfie smiled.

They took turns freshening up in the bathroom and

then, before they ventured outside, Tobias handed Alfie a knitted beanie he'd brought along. "You, uh, might want to cover your...." Not sure whether he was being insensitive, he touched the top of one of his own ears —rounded instead of pointed.

Luckily, Alfie didn't seem at all offended. In fact, he stroked the colorful wool. "It's a beautiful hat." He placed it carefully on his head.

Tobias felt his cheeks heat. "Thanks. I made it." He'd learned to knit during the pandemic because the idea of turning a long string into something useful had seemed a little like magic, and because it seemed a logical accompaniment to sewing. One of his few social activities was a Wednesday evening group stitch at a nearby yarn store. None of the other attendees seemed taken aback by his size, and he didn't feel awkward conversing about patterns and colorways and fibers. The event was on hiatus for the holidays, however, and now he wondered if he'd ever get to return.

Alfie, who—predictably—looked handsome in the hat, was beaming at him. "You have so many talents." And he didn't seem to intend any sarcasm.

When they stepped outside, Tobias was even more grateful he'd brought the hat. It was cold, and a few stray snowflakes danced through the light of the streetlamps. Although Tobias was fairly impervious to frigid temperatures, the last thing he wanted was Alfie getting a chill.

They walked slowly, Alfie leaning heavily on

Tobias's arm but not complaining. "This place reminds me a bit of home," he said wistfully.

"You have mountains?"

"Mine is the Kingdom of the Five Sisters, each of which is a snowy peak. According to legend, they were once women—not blood sisters, but close friends. When they grew old, they persuaded a wizard to turn them into mountains so that they could remain together. When storms blow winds down the slopes and into the valleys, we say that the sisters are laughing together over a private joke. Sometimes they rumble and belch ashes, and then we say they're arguing."

They reached the front door of a place called Black Bart's, which was unsurprisingly done up in a mild stagecoach-bandit theme overlaid with Christmas decorations. There were only a few other customers, and the teenage girl who seated them looked thoroughly bored.

Alfie, however, was fascinated and kept twisting around to take in his surroundings, even though doing so clearly hurt. He exclaimed quietly over the old photos, the spurs and other horsey paraphernalia hanging on the walls, and the battered old piano in the corner. His eyes grew huge over the menu, which offered a fairly pedestrian array of steaks, burgers, sandwiches, and salads. "So many options! Will you order for me, please?"

That was more responsibility than Tobias felt

comfortable with. "I don't know what you like and don't like."

"I'm sure I'll enjoy whatever you have."

What Tobias ended up ordering was a bowl of chicken noodle soup with bread rolls, an enormous bacon cheeseburger with fries, and a peppermint milkshake. It was a lot—he knew that. But he was a big guy, plus he figured he couldn't be blamed for wanting to drown his troubles in calories. Not after the day he'd had.

To his surprise, not only did Alfie avoid any snide comments about the quantity of food, he matched Tobias pretty much bite for bite, making appreciative noises as he went. "You're staring," Alfie said with a good-humored glint in his eyes.

"I'm admiring your ability to enjoy a meal."

"This is an excellent one. And it will help with my healing."

That reminded Tobias of his mother, who used to insist that a good meal would cure almost all of Tobias's ills. And maybe she'd been right. He rarely caught whatever virus was making the rounds, and when everyday mishaps resulted in scrapes or bruises, he was good as new within a day or so. Even his broken arm had healed fast enough to surprise the doctor.

They were both so busy eating that they didn't discuss anything of consequence, which was honestly a relief. Tobias could almost pretend they were on a date. Alfie was certainly good company—funny and bright and interested in everything he saw. He charmed the waitress too, seemingly without effort, and she ended up bringing them an order of onion rings on the house because, she said, they were such appreciative eaters.

But Tobias couldn't continue to ignore the troll-related elephant in the room. While he and Alfie waited for slices of what the waitress assured them was the best chocolate cake in Siskiyou County, Tobias did what he had to do. "Are you ready to tell me about Kol and Snjokarl?"

Alfie nodded glumly as he toyed with his fork. "I suppose so. You've been patient with me, and you're certainly entitled to hear the rest. Snjokarl is a prince as well, in the much larger and wealthier kingdom to our south. It makes him a powerful elf indeed, even though he has two older sisters and is therefore not the heir. I believe that since he cannot inherit the crown, he exerts his influence elsewhere."

"Like on Kol."

"Just so. My brother sees him simply as an ally, not a threat, and that's been another point of contention between us. In any case, Snjokarl has done an excellent job of whispering in Kol's ear and undermining everything my father attempted with him." Alfie twisted his fork hard enough to bend it, then looked chagrined and set it down. "Where once Kol was only mildly interested in leaving the empire, now he's become fixed on the idea. Obsessed, really."

Tobias nodded. "Snjokarl radicalized him."

"I suppose—" Alfie tensed suddenly, his wide-eyed gaze fixed on something over Tobias's shoulder.

CHAPTER

SEVEN

Tobias twisted around and saw two large men entering the dining room. Well, one large man—who looked to be as big as Tobias— and one *enormous* one. Tobias guessed they were in their seventies, and both were dressed in jeans and flannel. The comparatively smaller one had a long white ponytail and was clean-shaven, while the giant had an unwieldy cloud of steely curls and an impressive grizzled beard. He looked like Paul Bunyan's grandfather. Both of them seemed robust despite the gray hair and wrinkles, and they had stopped in their tracks to stare back at Alfie and Tobias.

Heart racing, Tobias leaned toward Alfie and attempted to whisper. "Is that guy a troll?"

Frowning, Alfie shook his head. "He resembles a snjómaður, but not... exactly." He didn't appear alarmed, which was good. Tobias remembered that snjómaður meant yeti, and that Alfie had said they weren't dangerous. But still.

The newcomers marched over to Tobias and Alfie's table. "What are you?" demanded the maybe-yeti.

But then his companion elbowed him. "That's kind of rude, Jerry." He smiled. "Forgive us, gentlemen. We spend a lot of time in the forest. Sometimes we sort of forget how to act civilized."

Even though Tobias was still trying to process this interaction, Alfie was unfazed. "It was a reasonable question. I was wondering the same of you, in fact. Forgive me for not standing and introducing myself properly. I've had a leg injury and prefer to remain seated."

"Don't worry about it. We—"

"I'm Jerry," the giant interrupted. He had a slight southern accent. "This is my partner, Art. Are you here to create any trouble?"

Alfie shook his head. "We're simply passing through."

By now, Tobias was slightly annoyed. "Are you guys cops or something? Because no offense, but you're a little, uh...."

"Old," Art finished for him with a chuckle. "Yep. And no, not cops. But Jerry was Forest Service—he's retired now—and I'm retired from the Bureau of Trans-Species Affairs. We used to be law enforcement adjacent, and I guess we haven't quite kicked the habit."

Although Tobias had never heard of the weird-sounding bureau, it was a relief to know that he wasn't the subject of a manhunt due to what had happened in Portland. At least not yet. "We're having a quiet dinner, after which we're heading back to our hotel room and going to sleep. We'll be gone by morning."

Jerry and Art exchanged looks, then Art nodded. "Look, your business is, well, none of our business. But your friend here says he's hurt. If you need some help, we still know people in the Bureau who can help. Part of the Bureau's responsibility is to assist non-human sentients when they're in trouble."

Non-human sentients?

Before Tobias could ask for more details, Alfie spoke up. "I thank you. But Tobias is assisting me wonderfully, and in any case my problems... well, let's say they exist in a realm well outside the Bureau's jurisdiction."

Art shrugged. "Fair enough. We'll let you eat in peace. I see that Camila's about to bring you some chocolate cake. You're gonna enjoy that."

As the waitress approached the table, Art nodded and headed toward a vacant table near one of the windows. Jerry, however, stayed put and then, grinning, pointed at his foot. The biggest foot Tobias had ever seen. "Half," Jerry said. "On my father's side. You?"

Alfie tugged off his hat, revealing his pointed ears and making Jerry guffaw. "I'll be darned. Well, I guess it's the season." Jerry turned his attention to Tobias. "What about you?"

"I'm just an ordinary man."

"Huh. Well, all right. You two take care." He gave them a salute before trundling off to join his partner.

Camila, of course, had also seen Alfie's ears, but she simply shrugged. She set down the plates. "Enjoy!" she said and sailed away.

The cake was as wonderful as promised, but Tobias was too distracted to fully appreciate it. "Are there lots of, um, non-human sentients? Like... I don't know." He did a quick mental inventory of various movies and books. "Dragons and goblins and unicorns and merfolk and... and vampires and—"

"I don't know. This is your world, not mine." Alfie licked some frosting off his fork, which almost distracted Tobias from his distraction. "We know quite a bit about you, just as you do about us, but I imagine both sides are stuffed with myths and misconceptions. I wish I'd had the opportunity to explore your world under happier circumstances."

Tobias was going to pursue this, but he noticed—belatedly—that Alfie looked a little drawn. "Are you ready to head back?"

"I think so."

After Tobias paid, he helped Alfie to his feet and provided an arm for support. It was a little selfish of him, how much he liked performing this role for Alfie. It made him feel useful and as if his size was finally a benefit instead of an embarrassment.

And speaking of size, Art and Jerry watched as Tobias helped Alfie toward the exit. Alfie waved good-

bye at them and they both waved back. But Alfie and
Tobias had taken only a few steps outside when Jerry
rushed through the door, moving with unexpected
speed for someone his age and size. "Are you sure you
don't want to get in touch with the Bureau? They saved
my ass, a long time ago."

"I'd prefer to have as few people involved as possible." The way Alfie said it, Tobias found it easy to
believe he was a prince.

Jerry shrugged. "Suit yourself." He squinted down
at Tobias. "Are you *sure* you're entirely human? I
could've sworn…. Well, never mind. Can I give you
boys some advice?"

"I'd be honored, sir," said Alfie.

"When things get rough, nothing beats having a
good partner. Keep close to each other, you know? And
happy holidays."

Jerry patted each of them on the shoulder—Alfie
gently but Tobias almost hard enough to make him
stagger—and then ambled back into Black Bart's.

"I've never truly had a partner, for anything," Alfie
said as he and Tobias shuffled back to the motel. "I've
had friends, of course. Lovers. But when I was younger
I was too wayward to be interested in accomplish-
ments, and when I grew older, I was too proud to enlist
help, I suppose. Too shortsighted. Perhaps things
would have gone differently if I hadn't insisted on
confronting Kol by myself." He stopped in his tracks,
still clutching Tobias's arm, shivering a little in the
cold.

"What's wrong?"

"None of this is fair to you. Nobody asked whether you wanted this role. You've been put in danger and forced to flee your home. You've—"

"I want this role."

Tobias stated that with a sureness that surprised even him. Maybe he wasn't being especially rational, but rationality might not be the best choice when your whole world has turned upside down. Anyway, he felt what he felt, and he wanted to help Alfie. He couldn't recall wanting anything so desperately, in fact.

Alfie was staring at him as if Tobias—even though not an elf prince—was the remarkable one. "I'm just a data engineer," Tobias protested.

"You're not 'just' anything."

It was a short walk back to their room, but by the end, Tobias was nearly carrying Alfie. Inside, Alfie sank heavily onto the bed and didn't protest as Tobias removed his borrowed coat, sneakers, and socks. "How's your leg? And your bruises?"

"Better."

Alfie must have realized that Tobias didn't believe him, so he peeled off his flannel shirt and tee, revealing a pale chest still mottled with discolorations. They were less horrifying than they'd been the day before, however, and the tattoos were extra swirly. He managed to wiggle out of the borrowed sweatpants and unwrapped the bandage on his leg. The wound had closed already and there was no sign of infection, although everything was scabby and slightly swollen. "See?"

"You do heal quickly."

"An advantage of being an elf. I'm going to end up with a scar, of course, but that's fine. And now I owe you the rest of my tale. Will you join me in bed to hear it?"

Bed. Yes. The one and only bed, which was plenty big enough for the two of them despite Tobias's size. Alfie was currently climbing under the covers. Naked. Apparently Tobias was trapped in a romance trope after all.

He swallowed, said, "Um, I need a minute," and rushed off to the bathroom.

It was a tiny space, with both a mirror and a shower that forced him to stoop. He glared at his reflection as he whispered, "You faced *trolls* today. You can manage an overnight with a nude elf." Unconvinced, he took his time getting ready for bed. Maybe if he dawdled long enough, Alfie would be asleep when Tobias emerged.

Except Tobias really did need to hear the rest of the Kol story, which he already knew wouldn't end happily.

Alfie was still wide awake and looking amused when Tobias stepped out of the bathroom. "You must be very clean by now."

Tobias simply stood there, feeling huge and awkward and stupid.

"Is everything all right?" asked Alfie.

There was no way to answer that without *sounding* awkward and stupid. So instead Tobias stripped as quickly as possible, leaving on his boxer briefs, and dove under the blankets. He stared up at the ceiling rafters as if they might offer suggestions on how not to be a dork.

Alfie switched off the bedside light. "You are a beautiful man," he said softly.

"In the dark, sure."

"Elves have excellent night vision."

"Look, you don't have to—"

"Beautiful," Alfie repeated firmly and stroked Tobias's cheek with a single warm finger. "And don't argue with me about it. My family is renowned for our exacting and exquisite taste in aesthetics. Even Kol can't be criticized in that regard."

Right—Kol. Who was way more important right now than the fact that Alfie's touch made Tobias burn, made his skin feel too tight, made him want to lose himself forever in Alfie's embrace.

"Tell me about Snjokarl, please."

Alfie sighed deeply enough to shake the mattress. "As you said, he radicalized Kol. He's not merely persuasive—he's dangerous as well. Most of the empire's trolls live in his kingdom and are faithful to him. He uses them as guards and... thugs."

"And you said trolls can cross over from one world to the other."

"Yes. And in addition to being strong, they are excellent trackers. They can find almost anything or anyone if they set their minds to it. They would be a formidable force on their own if they were numerous, but luckily for the rest of us, their belligerent temperaments—off-putting to even their own kind—have kept their population small and prevented them from unifying."

Trackers. Well, that explained how the trolls had found Alfie at Tobias's house. Horrifyingly, it also suggested that they'd discover him wherever he went. All the more reason to talk to Aunt Virginia, since Tobias couldn't think of anyone else who could possibly help.

But wait. "If they're so great at finding stuff, how come they didn't discover you for... I don't know how long? Decades."

"Because I was inanimate. Once the enchantment was removed and I was once again a living being, they found me straight away."

"Oh." Tobias supposed that made some sense. "Sorry—I interrupted your story. What happened after Snjokarl got to Kol?"

Another sigh from Alfie. "Father became ill, and as he weakened, Kol exerted his own power more often. He and I argued more violently. Perhaps it would have been better had I held my temper and tried to counter

Snjokarl's effects, but I'm not patient. And honestly, I feared what would happen to our kingdom when Father died. I belatedly realized that I needed allies—partners—but also realized that if I recruited my friends to support me, there was a strong possibility that they'd be prosecuted for treason once Kol had the crown."

"You must have felt so alone."

"Isolated and terrified. And not making rational choices. I should have fled the kingdom, but I couldn't bear the thought of abandoning my father as he lay dying."

In the heavy silence that followed, something occurred to Tobias. "You haven't mentioned your mother."

"My mother was a member of one of the wild clans that live in the far north, outside the empire's boundaries. They are few in number. They want nothing to do with any form of governance, and they rarely interact with outsiders. I'm told she traveled south out of youthful curiosity, met the ruler of the Kingdom of the Five Sisters, and... had a fling. A bit of a protracted one. She promised the king she would give him two children as long as he promised that after she left, neither he nor their offspring would ever try to contact her. She returned to her homeland a few months after I was born."

Tobias considered that for a moment. "Did that make you sad?"

"Not especially. My father loved me and I was well cared for. I never knew her, so I didn't miss her."

That made sense. Tobias had never minded not having a father. "I'm sure your father appreciated having you there when he was ill."

"He did, and despite everything, I don't regret staying at his bedside. His mind was muddled at the end, but he knew that I was there and told me he loved me."

Alfie sounded a little choked up, so Tobias reached over to pat his shoulder consolingly. Somehow, however, Alfie ended up snuggled up against him, head tucked into the crook of Tobias's arm and soft hair tickling Tobias's cheek. It felt lovely.

Maybe Alfie thought so too, because he gave a little wiggle, settling more comfortably into position, and this time his sigh sounded contented rather than heavy. "You don't mind?"

"Not a bit."

"Mmm. Perfect." He wiggled again. "It's much easier to talk about unpleasant things when I'm near you like this. You are a bulwark against sorrow. Father died. Kol immediately began making plans to withdraw from the empire. Which would quite likely result in a war, but he didn't seem concerned about that. He demanded that at his coronation I publicly state my endorsement of his ideas. I refused. We had the biggest fight yet, which is when I finally recognized the truth I'd been avoiding: that he would kill me over this. My own brother. So *then* I fled. But it was too late. He sent Snjokarl after me."

Alfie shuddered and Tobias held him more tightly. "Too chicken to go after you himself?"

"Snjokarl likely requested the task. He hates me because I opposed him. And he's a sadistic wretch. Anyway, I went north, hoping to leave the kingdom, but Snjokarl's trolls caught me before I reached the border and dragged me to him. I like to think that my brother's instructions were to kill me straight away, and that the torture was Snjokarl's personal addition."

"He *tortured* you?" Appalled, Tobias clutched Alfie even more tightly, until he realized that might be painful and relented a bit.

Ironically, Alfie ended up comforting Tobias. "Only a little," he said, stroking Tobias's arm. "I managed to escape my bonds before he got too far. I tried to get out of the palace where he held me, but one of his trolls found me. I'm not much of a fighter even at my best, and I knew it was a lost cause, but I struggled anyway because what else could I do? Better to die quickly during an escape attempt than slowly at Snjokarl's hands. The troll... he had a knife. That's how my leg was injured. And then...." He trailed off into silence.

"It's a terrible memory. You don't have to talk about it anymore." Tobias figured he'd heard all the important parts anyway. Not that he really had a handle on how Alfie had ended up in this world, and as a doll to boot. He also had no clue how Alfie might escape his pursuers. But he hoped Aunt Virginia could help with that.

"It's not that I don't want to say more, Tobias. I

can't, because I don't really remember what happened. There was a lot of shouting. A burst of light? And then... then I was in your house and I *hurt* and I thought you were a troll. I'm sorry about that part."

"I've seen trolls now, and I know what I look like. I can understand your confusion."

Alfie yawned noisily, which made Tobias yawn too. It wasn't especially late, but they'd had a trying day, and Tobias wanted to get an early start. His eyelids felt heavy. And Alfie was so warm and sweet against him, so *comfortable*, as if the two of them had been made to lie like this. Also, he smelled remarkably like the peppermint milkshake that Tobias had enjoyed with dinner.

"We'll get to San Francisco tomorrow and we'll figure this out," Tobias promised. "I won't let Snjokarl get his claws on you again."

"My hero."

Those two good words floated around in Tobias's head and eventually followed him into sleep, where he dreamed of castles and kings and beautiful elves. They were good dreams.

When he awakened at dawn, Alfie was nowhere to be found.

Tobias's first, horrifying thought was that the trolls had whisked Alfie back to their world. It seemed unlikely they'd manage that without waking Tobias, but he'd seen a lot of strange things lately.

He was saved from hysterics when he noticed the piece of paper lying on top of his small suitcase. The paper had been torn from the motel notepad, and it contained a message written in spiky but legible cursive:

My dearest Tobias,

I am so sorry to do this to you. But I've put you in mortal danger. I cannot allow harm to come to you. The trolls will leave you alone if I'm not near you.

Thank you for being a true friend. You may think me foolish, but I do love you already despite our short time together. I'm grateful I've had the chance to love.

Yours always,

A

INSTEAD OF DISSOLVING INTO HYSTERICS, Tobias nearly threw a tantrum. With considerable effort, he got hold of himself and took a few deep breaths to clear his brain. "*Think*, Lykke," he said as he hastily pulled on his clothes. "Where the hell is an injured elf going to go at seven thirty in the morning?"

Of course, Alfie could have left hours ago. He'd said he had good night vision. That was too dismal to even consider.

Tobias gathered his few belongings and ventured out into the cold. His car was still there, so Alfie hadn't driven away; Tobias doubted he would have even known how. A glance up the empty street told him that none of the few shops or restaurants were open yet. Alfie could have hitched a ride out of town. Or he could be hiding somewhere in town, in a shed maybe, or even inside someone's house.

God, he could be anywhere.

"Think," he repeated, turning a slow circle in the little parking lot. Talking to himself was better than doing nothing at all, he hoped. Better than giving up and never seeing Alfie again. Spending the rest of his life wondering what had happened to him, picturing him being tortured and killed, picturing him all alone in either one of the two worlds.

Up the street, there was a clock tower on the building that housed a bank and the local newspaper. Tobias stopped, stared at it, and knew it was sending him a message. *Time.* Now was the time. He could live in denial and resign Alfie to his fate. Or he could allow himself to accept the truth... and just maybe have some hope of finding the elf who loved him.

"I am Tobias Hilmar Lykke," he said out loud. To the sleeping town. To the world at large. To himself. "I am the son of Isabella Lykke. I am the godson of Virginia Segreti, Countess of Contovello. I am a data engineer.

"And I am a troll."

CHAPTER

EIGHT

"I am a troll."

Tobias repeated it because saying it out loud was a surprising relief. Maybe because the sky didn't fall. Maybe because it could sometimes feel a lot better when you stopped lying to yourself.

He hadn't been entirely honest with himself for a long time.

Ever since he was very young, he'd known he was different. He tried to chalk that up to the obvious things: He was adopted. He didn't look anything like his mother. He was always bigger than everyone else his age. He was gay. All of that set him apart from many of his peers, but aside from the awkwardness of being oversized, he'd never minded any of it. He knew his mom loved him exactly as he was; she said so often, and it showed in her actions.

But he'd never asked her about his biological parents.

When he reached adolescence, she'd offered to discuss the details of his adoption more than once, but he'd nervously shied away from the topic. He didn't want to know where he'd come from because, deep in the back of his mind, he already knew: he'd come from somewhere very strange.

So Tobias and Denial had spent nearly three decades living together, and as far as he was concerned, the arrangement could have continued indefinitely.

Until an elf appeared in his home, leaving no more room for Denial.

When you collected data for a living, and you organized it and analyzed it, sometimes the conclusions were inescapable, no matter how unpleasant they might be. And Tobias had now collected a lot of data: His adopted status. His size. The difficulty with social connections. The fact that Alfie had at first believed him to be a troll. The glee he'd felt when battling the home-invading trolls—who'd at first assumed he was one of them. Jerry's conviction that Tobias was not an ordinary human.

Of course, this self-revelation raised a lot of new questions. Had his mother known what he was? How did she come to adopt him? What had happened to his biological parents? How had he even left the other world and gotten into this one? Was he destined to become ill-natured and violent? What did all of this mean for his future? And what would Alfie do if he found out?

Right *now*, however, only one question was important.

Where was Alfie?

If Tobias was a troll, he might as well embrace the useful aspects of his nature. Alfie had told him that trolls could track anyone.

So he took a few deep breaths of the cold mountain air, closed his eyes, and followed the steps he always used for a thorny work problem. First he pictured a blank computer screen. At the top of the screen he placed a tiny image of the beginning, which in this case was him right now, in the middle of a parking lot with his breath pluming and the sky above slowly lightening. At the bottom of the screen he imagined the end result: Alfie, safe in Tobias's arms. Now all he had to do was figure out the path between them.

When he was at work, that path consisted of numbers, computer code, and client specs. So what should it be now?

Elf. Christmas. Christmas tree. Tree!

Hadn't Alfie mentioned that the forest here reminded him of home? It made sense that he'd retreat to the woods, which would also allow him to avoid endangering innocent bystanders when Snjokarl's trolls arrived.

Alfie was in the forest; Tobias was sure of it. But they were surrounded by millions of acres of forest, and Tobias had no idea in which direction to set off. Plus, a substantial portion of this region had much rougher terrain than Tobias could handle. He hiked sometimes, but he wasn't an experienced mountaineer.

"That's fine," he reminded himself. "You know the general program to use. Now concentrate on the specifics."

His eyes remained closed, and as he focused on his steady heartbeat, another image began to appear on his mental screen. It was fuzzy at first but eventually clarified to Alfie sitting on the ground with his back against a tree, his knees drawn up and circled by his arms. He looked cold and lonely and miserable.

"Where?" Tobias murmured.

The screen cleared and was promptly replaced by a map depicting Siskiyou County. When Tobias zoomed in a little, a red circle appeared, exactly like when he searched for addresses on his phone. He continued to zoom in until the precise location was clear.

Alfie was five miles south, inside a state park and, thankfully, not far from the freeway.

Tobias took a few minutes to check out of the motel, then got into his car and zoomed out of town. He drove a lot faster than was legal or advisable, but there was very little traffic and the road was clear of ice and snow.

The lot at the state park was deserted. It was too early for most day use, and presumably, few people wanted to camp when the temperature was well below freezing. After parking in the spot farthest from the entrance and closest to where he knew Alfie sat, he took off down the trail.

He might be more of a plodder than a sprinter, but he could keep going for a long time. And while he *felt* the cold, it didn't bother him, didn't make him shiver, didn't make his skin chap. When he was little, his mother had fussed over him in winter, insisting that he wear warm coats, thick socks, and mittens. When it rained—which was often—she handed him umbrellas. But he'd always managed to lose the umbrellas and mittens, forget the coats at school, and wear holes in the socks. Eventually she'd accepted that he wasn't going to succumb to hypothermia, and she'd given up on protecting him from the elements.

Was cold tolerance part of being a troll? He had no idea, but whatever the reason, he was thankful for it now as he hurried toward Alfie.

Dim light filtered through the evergreen branches, and Tobias's tread was nearly silent on the needle-covered ground. He felt almost as if he had the world to himself. Under other circumstances, he would have quite enjoyed a jog in this place, where he wasn't in danger of being run over by an inattentive driver or splashed by a bus barreling through puddles. Maybe, if he survived this adventure, he should consider moving out of Portland, maybe getting a little place up on Mt. Hood. He did mostly remote work anyway, and it wouldn't be too terrible a commute if he didn't have to do it often.

If he survived.

He jogged for over fifteen minutes, following the route map in his head, until he came to a spot that was especially crowded with trees. One of them, recently fallen, blocked the trail. Instead of clambering over it, Tobias walked slightly downhill and past the root end. There was no path, but at least the underbrush was a little easier to get through during the winter. He'd gone perhaps a hundred yards when he spied a cedar with a particularly thick trunk.

That was the one. He was as certain as he was of his own name—and more certain than he was of his species.

Heart racing, Tobias rushed to the tree. Alfie cowered at the base on the other side.

"It's me!" Tobias announced as he collapsed to his knees beside Alfie.

Alfie's eyes grew wide. "T-T-Tobias?" His lips were blue and his teeth chattered.

"Yes!"

"N-not a troll?"

Best to sidestep that issue for the moment. "It's me, Alfie. Are you hurt? Hang on." Tobias took off his hoody, removed Alfie's too-thin coat, and put the hoody on him. Then he replaced the coat and wrapped him in his arms, sharing his warmth.

Alfie clutched him back and murmured into his neck. "But you can't— How did you—

You'll be cold, and the trolls, and how—"

"I'm fine. Can you walk back to the car? It's about a mile or so, I think."

Alfie feebly tried to pull away. "Go away, Tobias. You're not safe here."

"Neither are you."

"I'm not safe anywhere," Alfie snapped. "Didn't you read my note? You need to get far away from me before the trolls come again."

"I won't. Look, you come back with me to the car, or I'll stay here with you in the middle of the goddamn forest. I'd prefer the car. It's warm and we can drive to breakfast. But in any case, I'm not abandoning you."

For a moment, Alfie was silent, and then he sniffled against Tobias's shoulder. "It's stupid of you to stay with me."

"I never claimed to be brilliant. Now, come on. Can you walk okay?"

As it turned out, Alfie couldn't, at least not without Tobias's help. But he did his best, Tobias supported him as needed, and about half an hour later they were back at the parking lot. Tobias helped him into the passenger seat and buckled him in before getting into his own seat, starting the engine, and setting the heater to full blast.

Alfie leaned his head back and closed his eyes. "You weren't supposed to find me."

"I'm responsible for you— No, don't argue with me. I *am*. And it's a responsibility I accept willingly because I'm your friend." And because he was maybe falling in love with Alfie, but he didn't say so. No need to make the situation even more complicated.

Instead of answering, Alfie sighed.

Tobias drove out of the parking lot and merged onto the southbound freeway. He wanted breakfast but didn't want to backtrack into town. He'd find something, maybe in Redding, which was less than an hour away.

They'd traveled for five or six miles when Alfie spoke again. "How did you find me, Tobias?"

This was the part Tobias dreaded. Being a troll had come in handy when tracking down a missing elf. But the elf in question had a strong—and understandable —detestation of trolls. How would he react when he found out about Tobias? He'd be horrified, terrified, angry. And just the anticipation of that was enough to break Tobias's heart.

"Could we discuss this after we eat?" He could at least postpone the inevitable.

"All right."

They continued on for a while, the silence between them deafening. Finally, Tobias cleared his throat. "Will you promise me something, please?"

"I cannot promise your safety if you remain with me," Alfie replied wearily. "In fact, I can almost guarantee the opposite."

"I'm not asking for that. Look, I'm going to do my very best to get some answers and find a way to protect you permanently. This is something I *want* to do, okay? I'd be really upset if I didn't get a chance to at least try to help. So promise me you won't take off again without me—not until you're safe. Please."

Alfie reached over and set a hand on Tobias's leg, a gesture that already felt familiar. "Very well. I promise. And Tobias, if I had a choice—if not for trolls and

Snjokarl and Kol and... well, everything—I would remain at your side forever."

"You don't have to—"

"I have, erm, interacted with a goodly number of people over a variety of species. I told you I was wild, yes? But I have never met anyone who draws me as you do. It's not only that you are brave and handsome, although you are certainly both of those. When I am with you, food has more flavor. Colors are brighter. The scenery is more beautiful. Everything is simply *more* and infinitely better."

The freeway grew a little blurry, and Tobias had to blink rapidly to clear his vision. His throat felt tight. That cinnamon roll sensation was back, but at the same time a thousand tiny blades poked at his heart. Because he felt the same way about Alfie—inexplicably, completely in love—but it couldn't go anywhere. Even in the happiest of outcomes, in which they both survived, Alfie would be horrified when he found out that Tobias was a troll. There was also that little detail of them living, literally, in two different worlds.

"How about a sausage McMuffin?" he asked, knowing it was the most idiotic response ever to a poetic declaration of love.

Alfie didn't seem to mind, however. He chuckled and squeezed Tobias's leg. "I don't know what that is, but I'm sure it's delightful."

Multiple crises averted. For now.

CHAPTER
NINE

Alfie fell asleep soon after breakfast. That was mostly a relief, in that it meant Tobias could postpone the Big Trollhood Reveal. And Alfie's recovery from his nasty injuries also required the rest.

But it also meant that Tobias was mostly alone with his thoughts, and those thoughts weren't pretty. He'd never been the type to question his identity or his life path. He could probably thank his mother for that. She'd provided him a depth of love and support that instilled confidence in both himself and the future, despite his challenges with social interactions. *You're you*, had been her constant message, *and you are capable and worthy exactly as you are.*

Well, he'd appreciated that. He still did. But Mom wasn't around anymore and he had nobody else to discuss his self-revelations with.

What did it mean that he was a troll? Was he

destined to turn brutish and cruel? Did he have a place in this world anymore? If not, did he have a place in Alfie's?

Maybe Snjokarl's minions would kill him and he wouldn't have to worry about any of this.

"Are you all right?" Alfie sounded sleepy.

"Sure."

"You groaned."

Shit. "Just tired of being in the car. But we're getting pretty close. Would be only about an hour if traffic wasn't so awful."

Alfie sat up straighter and peered outside. "Are there always so many vehicles?"

"Not at this time of day, I don't think." Tobias considered for a minute. "Christmas is in two days and today is Monday. A lot of people probably have the week off and are on vacation or on their way to visit family."

Alfie didn't respond right away. Then he said, "Ah. On top of everything else, I'm making you miss your holiday celebrations."

Tobias couldn't help barking a laugh. "There's nothing to interrupt."

"I see. Which winter holiday do you observe?"

"None." Tobias was going to leave it at that, but then he feared that Alfie would ask how Tobias had managed to track him down. That story was definitely going to have to come out eventually... but not right this minute.

"Mom and I used to do several—Christmas,

Hanukkah, Kwanzaa, Solstice—but sort of in a low-key educational way. Like, we'd read some facts or folklore and eat something appropriate." Stated baldly like that, it likely sounded dumb, but he'd enjoyed it a lot as a kid. It was fun finding out the different ways that people made a day special.

"I think I like your mother very much."

That warmth returned to Tobias's chest. It was becoming almost familiar. "Mom was a professor, so she always had a few weeks off around now. We'd drive down to visit Aunt Virginia. We'd all dress up and she'd have a spectacular meal catered. Then the next day Mom and I would do a road trip. Sometimes it was a big deal like Disneyland, and sometimes it was just poking around small towns or stopping at every beach on the coast."

He hadn't really thought about those journeys for a long time, expecting the memories to be painful. It turned out, however, that they were more sweet than bitter.

"How about you?" he asked Alfie. "Do you have a winter holiday?"

Alfie was quiet for so long that Tobias thought he might have fallen asleep. But when he risked a quick glance to the passenger seat, Alfie was awake and staring ahead. Finally he spoke, but in a monotone unlike his usual animated style. "Traditionally, the king hosts a party on the longest night of the year. Everyone who can travels to the capital, and there are drinks and food and dancing until the sun rises.

There's a lot of sex too—it's that kind of night. When I was a child, however, my father would meet with Kol and me after the party—just after sunrise—in his private quarters. Just the three of us, you understand?"

"That didn't happen often because he was king?"

"Precisely. But that morning there were no advisors or courtiers or servants. We ate little bits of food left over from the party, and Father would tell us stories and listen as we talked about whatever boyhood fancies we had at the moment. He would tell us that he was proud of us. For an hour or two, we were... an ordinary family." Alfie heaved a heartbreaking sigh.

Tobias reached over for what he hoped was a comforting knee pat. Then he returned his attention fully to the road.

A few moments later, trying to keep his voice neutral, he asked, "Um, Alfie?"

"Yes?"

"Do trolls know how to drive?"

He was asking because a silver Dodge Ram had been riding his tail for the past several miles. It was fairly normal for California drivers to leave virtually no stopping distance between cars, but this guy was so close that the truck took up all of Tobias's rear window. And when Tobias had carefully switched lanes—three times now—the Ram had switched right along with him. The most recent time, it had cut off another car so boldly that it received a flurry of angry horns.

Alfie, who probably saw Tobias glancing repeatedly

into the rear-view mirror, twisted around in his seat—which must have hurt—and groaned. "Oh no."

"Trolls can *drive*?" Tobias was aware he sounded almost hysterical.

"If they spend enough time in your world."

Dandy.

For several minutes, while Alfie kept casting nervous looks behind them, Tobias tried to lose the Ram in traffic. But it was no good, and after the third near-accident, he started worrying that the trolls would cause a wreck. Innocent drivers on their way to Christmas at Grandma's didn't deserve to become troll-rage victims.

Unable to think of a better plan, Tobias took the next exit, which funneled him into the midst of farmland. He was dismayed but not surprised when the Ram followed.

"Shit."

"Tobias?"

"I'm in a car chase like a scene from a stupid movie. I've never been in a car chase before. I don't know what to do." Also, he drove a Kia Soul because it was practical and had been recommended on several websites as a good choice for tall drivers. If it had any evasive abilities, it hadn't come up in his online search. One good bump from behind by that huge pickup would probably do him in.

"I'm sorry. I don't know anything about cars. But I believe in you, Tobias. You are a hero."

The words might have been nothing more than

cheerleading, but they gave Tobias strength none-theless. He floored the gas and took off down the road, the Ram in hot pursuit. Luckily there was little traffic here, and Tobias was able to swerve around the few cars he did encounter. He briefly wondered what would happen if a cop car appeared, but since none did, there was no use speculating.

He made a sharp right onto a side road—so fast that he skidded a little—while the Ram raced forward along the original road. But the next time Tobias checked, the Ram had turned too and was barreling off-road to catch up with them. It even pulled up next to them and tried to force him off the road into a ditch, but Tobias was able to surge ahead and, a few seconds later, take another abrupt turn.

This put them on a narrow road with farmland on either side and, in the distance, some hills. There was no other traffic, which was a mixed blessing. On the one hand, it meant other drivers weren't in danger; on the other, there was nothing for Tobias to hide behind or to put between him and his pursuers. For the moment, all he could do was drive as fast as he could. Unfortunately, the Ram had no problems keeping up.

"They're going to make us crash," he growled.

"They won't want to kill me," replied Alfie, voice tight. "Yet. Snjokarl would be disappointed."

That didn't make Tobias feel any better.

The Ram pulled almost abreast and tried to run them off the road, but Tobias was able to surge forward and then, a short distance later, make a fast turn onto a wide gravel road. He heard the Ram skid when it tried to follow, but his relief was short-lived when the truck pulled out of the skid and accelerated. It was at this point that Tobias had a bit of a shock: the gravel road dead-ended after a couple of driveways. Those driveways led to farmhouses, which wouldn't do him any good. So he gave the wheel a desperate crank and managed to do a U-turn and rocket back down the gravel road and out onto the pavement. Behind him, he heard more skidding but saw only a thick cloud of dust kicked up by the tires.

Although the Ram had the advantage of sheer size and was as fast as his Kia, the Kia was more maneuverable and might fit into spaces that the bigger truck couldn't. If only he were able to find one of those spaces.

Well, at least he still had plenty of gas.

He continued down the road at top speed—trees, fields, and farmhouses nothing but blurs. After a few more random turns, the Ram was still in close pursuit.

"You're good at this," said Alfie.

"Lots of experience with driving simulation games." And to think he'd assumed he was just wasting his time with those. If he survived this, he was going to have to leave some games a five-star review.

Tobias slipped around a slow-moving farm truck and then, a mile or so later, an Amazon delivery van. He did another couple of turns and executed a peel-out that probably didn't do his tires any good but did succeed in getting a bit of space between him and the Ram, which made him whoop with delight.

He was having fun.

That thought was both shocking and inappropriate, but it was also true. He'd never had any real adventures, and now here he was with a gorgeous elf at his side, acting as if he was in a low-rent fantasy version of *Fast & Furious*. He wasn't fond of the life-threatening aspects, and he was enraged about the threats to Alfie… but he was also doing something a lot more interesting than moping through the holidays.

He was nearing a farmhouse perched on a hill when he saw a possible solution to his current problem. At the bottom of the hill was a muddy-looking pond. A fence ran between the pond and the road, with just a narrow strip of grassy ground on the pond side. There were a few overgrown shrubs there too, with lots of branches and no main trunk. Road, fence, and strip of ground were all several feet higher than the pond.

"Willing to take a risk?" he asked Alfie.

"Yes. I have faith in you."

Well. What more could Tobias ask for.

He suddenly veered off the road and onto the driveway that led to the farmhouse. But instead of continuing up the hill, he turned again—so fast that the Kia felt as if it might roll—and gunned it onto that little grassy space between pond and fence.

The Ram was right on his tail.

And a wide-ass shrub was dead ahead.

Another violent turn of the steering wheel and he

cleared the bush, just barely. Branches scraped the sides, undoubtedly wrecking his paint job, but he made it.

The troll driving the Ram must have realized at the last second that his vehicle was too wide. Tobias heard brakes squeal and metal crash, but he was too busy trying to get back to the road to see what had happened.

Alfie, however, let out a cheer. "You got him!"

Back on solid pavement, Tobias dared to stop and look behind. The Ram was upside down in the pond, the tires slowly spinning above the waterline.

He looked at Alfie, Alfie looked back... and they crashed into each other for a triumphant, messy, wonderful kiss.

CHAPTER
TEN

Kissing Alfie was one of the best activities Tobias could think of. But they'd just been involved in a car chase, they didn't know if the trolls had survived their trip into the pond, and in any case, Tobias didn't want to explain things to an irate farmer or the local sheriff.

So he pulled away from Alfie with considerable reluctance, put the car into gear, and headed back to the freeway that would take them to San Francisco.

"Are you okay?" he asked. "Your bruises didn't get banged up too bad?"

"That was magnificent."

Tobias wasn't sure whether Alfie meant his driving or the kiss and decided not to ask. Either way, it was a compliment. "I never thought I'd do that in real life."

"I'm sorry that I—"

"I'm not complaining. I enjoyed it. Honestly, it was even better than yesterday's fight."

He received one of Alfie's leg squeezes. Tobias was really starting to like those. They were so... affirming.

"The Emperor used to host annual sporting competitions," Alfie said. "Archery, wrestling, footraces... those sorts of things. Athletes could win prizes, and the kingdoms represented by the winners could brag about it. Occasionally, minor border disputes and trade negotiations were settled through the games. Much better than warfare."

Tobias figured this was something like the Olympics. "Did you participate?"

Alfie laughed. "No! I am not remotely talented enough. But I did attend as Father's representative, and it was great fun to watch. Of course there was also quite a lot of feasting, drinking, and fucking. They were wonderful events. But the reason I mention it is that you would make a worthy competitor."

"Me?" Now it was Tobias's turn to laugh. "I run slow and have no idea how to shoot arrows. Unless car racing is one of the contests, I wouldn't be much good."

"We don't have motor vehicles. But Tobias, I am certain that you would excel at anything you put your mind to. You are formidable. You've bested trolls twice in two days, and very few could say the same."

This would have been an excellent opening for Tobias to reveal his identity. But he kept his mouth shut.

Driving in San Francisco and the surrounding areas was almost as harrowing as racing trolls. The traffic was mostly stop-and-go, and the streets and freeways did unpredictable things like veering off in strange directions and splitting up in ways one wouldn't expect. But Alfie was enchanted by the Bay Bridge and fascinated by the city itself. "Look at those big ships!" he exclaimed. "And those buildings—they're so tall and shiny."

"No freighters or skyscrapers where you live?"

"We're far from the sea, and we live in modest buildings. Even the Royal Palace isn't—" Alfie stopped and sighed. "It's not especially grand, as palaces go. But it was my home."

"I'm sorry."

"And I apologize for being maudlin. I'm very grateful to be alive at all, and look what adventures I'm having! My life was never this interesting before."

Tobias had been thinking the same thing about his own life not that long ago. And *interesting* was an ambiguous term. Mysterious fungal infections could be interesting, as could that weird noise your car was making, or the letter you recently received from the IRS. He'd spent most of his life assuming that predictable and safe were better than interesting. But now he wasn't so sure.

"YOLO," he said out loud.

"Pardon?"

"It's something Aunt Virginia told me when I visited her last. Right before she gave me the box with you inside, in fact. It means *you only live once.* She was advising me to crawl out of my shell and live more fully."

Tobias maneuvered along the streets, carefully avoiding lost tourists and foolhardy pedestrians. He'd been to Aunt Virginia's condo only once in the past decade and had never driven there himself. But with his troll skills, he inherently knew the way. He wondered idly whether his magical tracking abilities took into account current road conditions the way Google Maps did, or whether he was simply routed the shortest way. That might be interesting to experiment with, someday. If he didn't die first.

"Tobias, may I ask you a question?"

"Of course." Tobias was a little distracted, watching people hanging off a cable car that was chugging up a hill. How did the city's lawyers let them get away with that?

"You said that when I was entrusted to you, I was, erm, a doll."

"Yeah. I mean, more of a figurine, I guess? Like a really nice Christmas decoration."

Alfie chuckled. "I'm glad I was of some use, at least. But I was wondering—how did you transform me back to life?"

"I didn't. I left you on my shelf and then the next day *crash!* There you were on my living room floor. Bleeding." A small wave of nausea hit him at the memory.

"And no wizards entered your house in the interim?"

Tobias shook his head. "Not that I know of. I don't actually know any wizards."

Alfie was silent for a few moments. "That's puzzling."

There was a lot of that going around in Tobias's life lately. He turned a corner, narrowly missing a jaywalking man with several Macy's bags in one hand and a cell phone in the other.

"Are you sure you didn't do anything to reanimate me?" asked Alfie. "Think carefully, please."

Tobias tried to remember every event from the moment he'd opened the shoebox, but it wasn't easy. "I unwrapped you and put you on the shelf. That was about it. The next day I worked until dinner. Then THC snickerdoodles."

"What is that?"

"Cookies. With, uh, cannabis." Then he added, in case Alfie didn't know, "A relatively mild psychoactive drug."

He felt a little embarrassed, although he didn't use the drug often or irresponsibly and didn't think that there was anything immoral about getting stoned now and then. It just felt sort of sad that he was eating weed cookies all by himself when most other people were out celebrating the season with friends or family.

Alfie put a hand on Tobias's arm. "You combined a sweet pastry with a mind-opening substance?"

"Um, yeah?"

"Many of our important magic rituals begin that way. What did you do next?"

They were at a seemingly endless red light behind a long line of other cars, which gave Tobias a chance to think. "TV. Legos. That's about—" He stopped and felt his cheeks heat even before he described his next actions. "I kinda admitted to you—doll you, I mean—that I was lonely. And... I said I wished you were real."

Alfie gasped and jerked his hand away as if he'd been burned.

"What's wrong?" Tobias turned his head to see Alfie staring at him, eyes wide and mouth slightly agape. His face was even paler than usual, but the tips of his ears had gone bright red. "Alfie?" Tobias was ready to pull over despite the horrendous traffic.

But then Alfie blinked a few times and shook his head, his expression deeply troubled. "I... I need a bit of time to... think."

This wasn't good, whatever it was. But someone was honking impatiently. "Should I continue driving to Aunt Virginia's? We're about ten minutes away."

"Yes. Please."

There was a thick and heavy silence between them now. Tobias's insides—instead of reminding him of a cinnamon roll—felt filled with gravel. The nasty kind that works its way into your shoes and hurts when you walk.

Aunt Virginia's building perched atop Russian Hill,

but after circling the nearby blocks several times, Tobias couldn't find a place to park. He eventually resorted to temporarily blocking someone's driveway in order to consult his phone, which directed him to a parking garage near Ghirardelli Square, several blocks away.

When he and Alfie emerged onto the street after stowing the car, he expected Alfie to pause and admire the view of the bay, which was very pretty. However, he was clearly too distracted to do more than glance at the water and then trudge alongside Tobias up the steep hill. Mindful of Alfie's injuries, Tobias walked slowly.

"That's her," he said, pointing to the building when they were a block away. It wasn't a particularly necessary piece of information, but the lack of talking was getting on his nerves.

Alfie didn't answer, but just a few steps later, he grabbed Tobias's arm and pulled him to a halt. "I need to tell you something." Judging from Alfie's expression, it wasn't a good something.

Well, if they were going to be discussing bad shit, Tobias might as well fess up. He owed Alfie his honesty. "Me too." It was as good a spot as any, with that nice view below them. To their side was a low concrete railing with a steep drop-off on the other side. If Alfie was too horrified, maybe he'd push Tobias over the edge. At least hitting the hard ground below would be a softer landing than experiencing Alfie's rejection.

"May I go first?" When Tobias responded with a

nod, Alfie sighed. "This is... very difficult. But I must ask...." He swallowed loudly. "There is a magical ritual that some of my people engage in around the time of the winter solstice. They eat pastries and drink a special tea that causes temporary mental fogginess and sometimes hallucinations. They build elaborate constructions out of clay and twigs—these are meant to help concentrate the will. They watch short dramatic reenactments of historical events. And then they express their hearts' deepest desire in hopes that it will come to pass."

Uh oh. That sounded remarkably like Tobias's evening with the snickerdoodles and Legos. "And?" Tobias prompted, throat thick.

"And often their wishes are granted."

"Is that a bad thing?"

Alfie paused for a moment. He looked so delicate in his too-large borrowed clothes, standing on a sidewalk so far from his home, his pale hair tousled by the breeze. Tobias wanted to wrap his arms around him and protect him from everything. He wanted to see those blue eyes sparkle when they were trained on him, that generous mouth spread in a wide grin, and feel those long-fingered hands cradling his neck.

"The ritual is intended to find people a mate," Alfie said softly. "If the conjuring is successful, the supplicant will find their true love."

Appalled, Tobias gaped. "I trapped you in a love spell? Oh my God, Alfie, I didn't mean—"

Alfie quieted him with a hand. "No, no. You've done

nothing of the kind. The spell doesn't force anyone to do anything, and it doesn't construct love where none previously existed. It simply draws to the supplicant the individual who is their best possible match."

Tobias let out a relieved breath. "So I didn't enchant you or anything."

"You did not. Quite the opposite, in fact. Your actions resulted in returning me to my living state, for which I am deeply grateful."

"Then why did you look so horrified?"

"On your behalf. Because you had no notion what you were doing, and now it turns out that your best match is me. An elf who has nothing to offer you except danger, who comes from an entirely different world, who will soon be taken by trolls and...." He glanced away, but then turned back. "You deserve so much better."

Oh God. Neither cinnamon rolls nor gravel were inside Tobias now. Nope—he had a full-fledged cyclone in there, just like in *The Wizard of Oz*, complete with cows, nasty neighbors on bicycles, and other debris.

He took a deep breath and let it out slowly.

"Alfie, there is nobody I'd rather have than you. I don't care about the magic or... or fated mates, or whatever the deal is. If I could have you even for a short time, I'd consider myself the luckiest guy in two worlds."

A smile bloomed slowly on Alfie's face and he blinked away tears. But when he took a step toward

Tobias, arms raised, ready for an embrace, Tobias stopped him with a raised hand. "But there's something you have to know," said Tobias.

"Yes?"

Tobias took a deep breath and said the four hardest words of his life: "I am a troll."

CHAPTER
ELEVEN

I am a troll.

Even though Tobias and Alfie were out in the open, the words seemed to echo ominously around them, like thunder rolling in just before a storm. Alfie looked as if he'd been shot, and Tobias felt pretty much the same way.

Except for a teeny-tiny part of him that cheered silently, because finally he'd acknowledged who he was and what had set him apart from others for his whole life. He wasn't just a weird guy who didn't try hard enough to socialize with others. He was... something special?

But that meant he was apparently also inclined to be thuggish and cruel. And now the elf he'd fallen for looked both terrified and devastated, and Tobias didn't want any of that. The little cheering voice shut the hell up.

With visible effort, Alfie straightened his back and

lifted his chin. "You can congratulate your master for me. This was an especially devious form of torture."

"My mas— No! I'm not working for Snjokarl. I've never met him and had never even heard of him until you told me. And I'd never harm you."

Alfie's eyes were as cold as ice floes. "You've been lying to me for days. I don't believe you now."

Shit. This was even worse than Tobias had feared. "I haven't been lying. I didn't realize it myself until this morning."

"How could you not know you are a *troll*?" Alfie spat.

"Because I didn't even know trolls fucking existed!" Tobias roared back. "As far as I knew, they only existed in fairy tales and Tolkien's Middle-earth."

Alfie didn't respond, but perhaps his expression softened a tiny bit.

Tobias lowered his voice to a more reasonable, less troll-like volume. "I told you that I'm adopted. I never knew anything about my birth family, and I certainly wouldn't have suspected that they weren't human. I've spent my whole life here, remember? Among boring, ordinary people." He spread his arms to indicate the world as a whole—although maybe San Francisco wasn't the best place to make this point. On the other side of the street, a person in light-up bunny ears and a tutu was descending the hill, arm in arm with a person wearing assless chaps, a fluorescent-green G-string, and a crop top. In late December.

After a few more moments of silence, Alfie

slumped. "All right. But now that you do know, are you taking me to Snjokarl?"

"No!" This time Tobias was even louder. "I may be a troll but I'm not a monster. I care about you. I want to help you, and my identity has nothing to do with that."

"But trolls don't—" Alfie stopped himself. "I'm sorry. I don't know what to do with this information."

"I get it. Imagine how I feel." Tobias crossed his arms. He understood why Alfie felt so negative about trolls. Tobias had very few good thoughts about them himself. But there wasn't anything he could do to change who he was, and Alfie needed to understand that this wasn't exactly easy on Tobias either.

And, speaking of trolls, standing out here arguing wasn't the best idea. They might be attacked at any moment.

Tobias took a calming breath. "Look. We came here to get answers from Aunt Virginia. Let's go do that, okay? Maybe she can find a safe place for you, and then you won't have to deal with me anymore."

The corners of Alfie's mouth tightened, but he turned and continued up the hill, his gaze trained on his feet.

Tobias felt like shit. This was hardly the first time he'd been shunned or rejected, but those things didn't usually happen at the hands of someone he cared about. He didn't blame Alfie, but it still hurt.

A DIFFERENT CONCIERGE was on duty this time: a young person with a pixie haircut and an ugly Christmas sweater that coordinated nicely with the ugly Christmas decorations in the lobby. After hearing Tobias's request, the concierge narrowed their eyes at him and Alfie. "The Countess of Contovello does not entertain visitors."

Tobias heaved a sigh. "I know. But I'm her family and this is an emergency. Please tell her that Tobias is here, and—"

"Your name's not on the guest list. When residents are expecting guests, they let me know so the guests are on my list."

"Right. But I like I said, this is an emergency. If you could just call her—"

"That is not our policy."

Before Tobias could tell them exactly what they could do with their policy, Alfie stepped forward and turned on his most engaging smile. "You'll have to excuse Tobias. You know how trolls are. But it's quite urgent that we speak with the countess. It's a life-and-death matter."

Nobody could have resisted that charm, and the concierge looked as if they might be starting to bend. "But we have a policy. It protects our residents' privacy."

"Of course, and that's an admirable goal. Your employers must be very pleased with your diligence. It's nearly Christmas, however. The countess is alone.

I'm sure you wouldn't want to ruin her only opportunity to see family this season."

"No, of course not. But I—"

"Just call her, please. I am certain she'll be thankful that you did." There was just a hint of imperative in Alfie's manner that allowed Tobias to clearly see that he was indeed a prince.

Maybe the concierge saw that too, because they visibly conceded. "All right, I'll call. But I can't guarantee she'll want to see you."

Honestly, Tobias wasn't too positive about that either, but this was the best he could do. He watched nervously while the concierge picked up the phone, murmured into it, and after a pause, looked surprised at the response. "You can go up. Apartment 14C."

Alfie bowed to the concierge.

As they waited for the elevator, Tobias spoke quietly. "You were good at convincing them."

"Diplomacy has always been one of my few true skills. Even though it failed me with Kol."

The elevator arrived, but when they got in, Alfie seemed confused. "What is this? An anteroom?"

Tobias pushed the button. "An elevator. It—"

"Elevator! So they're real? I've always wished I could ride in one."

"Now's your chance."

The car started to rise, and although it did so smoothly, Alfie gasped and clutched Tobias's arm—then realized what he'd done and let go. That tiny drama made Tobias so sad he wanted to cry. But he kept his jaw set and eyes dry, and when they reached the fourteenth floor, he stepped out without waiting to see whether Alfie followed. If Alfie got stuck, that would be his own damned fault.

Alfie didn't get stuck. He followed Tobias down the hallway and waited with him after Tobias knocked.

"Do enter!" called a familiar voice.

Everything was exactly the same as his visit several days ago, except now the air carried faint whiffs of cinnamon and balsam. Maybe Aunt Virginia had Christmas decorations tucked away somewhere.

She was not in the parlor, which was as dark as ever, but her voice carried from another room. "Do sit down, my boy. I'll be there momentarily."

"I brought, um, a guest." He was met with silence.

Eventually, she said, "Whom have you brought?" He couldn't tell whether she was angry.

Tobias glanced at Alfie but couldn't read his expression in the gloom. "Alfred Clausen, second son of Claus Clausen. Um, King Claus Clausen, I guess." And then he added, because why the hell not, "He's an elf."

Aunt Virginia came bursting into the room and strode past them much faster than Tobias would have expected from someone in her nineties. She flung open the nearest drapes, flooding that part of the room with sunlight and illuminating her appearance: tan slippers, emerald-colored silk pajama trousers, and a nubbly gray sweater. Her hair, straight and almost transparent, fell to her waist; she wore no makeup.

Alfie gasped and executed such a deep bow that he bent nearly double. "My Lady."

After a moment of standing there stupidly, Tobias remembered his manners. "Thank you for seeing us, Aunt Virginia. This is Prince Alfred. Alfie, this is the Countess of Contovello."

"Forgive me, My Lady, but you are the most stunningly beautiful person I have ever met. Please excuse me if I am somewhat tongue-tied."

It was clear that Alfie wasn't lying or offering false flattery—he genuinely appeared awestruck. Tobias was... well, a little jealous. Not that he had any right to be, he reminded himself. And he ought to be thankful that Aunt Virginia had let them in, especially since she seemed the only reasonable source of answers to his many questions.

Which reminded him.

"Aunt Virginia, did you know that I'm a troll?" Without him intending it, a bit of annoyance came through.

Instead of scolding him for his rudeness, she gave a small sigh. "Toby dear, would you please bring in another chair for your friend?" She waved toward the parlor door that led to the kitchen.

Although Tobias could have protested that Alfie was not his friend and pretty much detested him, he kept his mouth shut and hurried into the kitchen, which hadn't changed one bit since he was a child. It was a very ordinary room, with those white laminate cabinets that had been so popular in the 80s. A bowl of apples sat on the counter, and there was an old console TV on a stand near the dinette set. An ache stabbed through him as he remembered sitting at that table with a glass of milk and a piece of fancy cake, leafing through a comic book while the grown-up talk washed over him like warm waves.

He grabbed one of the chairs and carried it back to the parlor, where Aunt Virginia and Alfie stood and silently stared at each other. When she took her customary seat, Alfie sat in the kitchen chair, and Tobias, as usual, got the inquisition chair.

Then everyone began to speak at once, a cacophony of questions, until Aunt Virginia held up her hand. "Please, boys. One at a time. And I shall claim privilege of the eldest and ask first. Tobias, how did you manage to return Prince Alfred to his true form?"

"Before I answer, you should know that some nasty trolls are after us. They've tried to get us twice, and they can track Alfie anywhere."

She waved a hand. "They cannot enter here. I am sorry to hear you've faced such difficulties. It seems, however, that you have overcome them."

"Tobias saved me," said Alfie, maybe a little reluctantly. "He's strong."

"Indeed. Tobias?"

He told her the brief story, THC snickerdoodles and all, and she nodded as he spoke. "Olve tried many times," she said when he was done. "But he was unable to restore the prince. I do apologize on his behalf, Your Highness."

"It's Alfie," he said, shaking his head. "And I think Tobias saved my life."

Everyone was being very polite, but Tobias wanted to scream. He clutched the arms of the chair hard enough to make them creak. "Aunt Virginia, can you please tell us what the hell happened? And how my mom ended up adopting a troll? And how Alfie can stay safe?"

"Very well. But before I begin, Tobias Hilmar Lykke, you must understand one thing very clearly: your mother loved you. She was proud of you. And she never once regretted that you were her son."

He'd been trying to appear stern, but now he sniffled. "Thank you."

"But he's a troll!" Alfie interjected, and then looked sorry he'd said anything.

Aunt Virginia fixed him with a glare that made him wilt. "*I* believe that the measure of a person lies not in their ancestry but rather in their actions. Tobias is smart and kind and loyal. He was a loving son who respected his mother and, when she took ill, set everything aside to care for her. He works hard. He has always made the effort to respect my eccentricities and to let me know I am in his thoughts. To the best of my knowledge, he has never harmed anyone unless necessary. He is my godson, and I would argue that he is equal to or better than any troll, human, *or* elf."

Because Tobias had to look away and blink hard, he

didn't see how Alfie responded. In any case, he had Aunt Virginia's esteem, and that meant the world to him.

With a final scowl in Alfie's direction, she began. "All right then. The tale begins shortly before my second marriage."

TWELVE

As you know, Tobias, my first husband was an artist and quite a few years my senior. Unfortunately, he died young, leaving me a youthful widow. I missed him deeply. I still do. But in December of 1953 I was visiting a bookstore that had recently opened. I thought I might purchase some books as a holiday gift for my dear friend Dorothy. Your grandmother, Tobias, and I am so sorry that you two never had a chance to meet.

When I arrived, I discovered that they were doing a poetry reading. Kerouac, perhaps? I can't recall for certain. I stayed to listen and, while I was there, met a fascinating man named Olve Lange. We went out for coffee. Then dinner. Then drinks. By the time we parted, it was very late and I knew I was in love.

We saw each other every day for a week. We went to parks, to the cinema, to galleries and museums. We had wild sex—well, you don't want to hear about that,

I'm sure. I adored my first husband, but I'd never felt as closely connected to him as I did with Olve.

The one problem between us, however, was that while I had told him every detail of my past, he'd shared almost nothing of his. I didn't push—I assumed he'd experienced something painful. But it's difficult to have a true relationship if both parties aren't open about the important things.

Olve and I went to Ocean Beach. We sat on a blanket I'd brought and he told me the most extraordinary tale. He said that he was from a world similar to this but not identical, that he was a wizard, and that he'd come here some years ago to study our world. He'd grown quite enamored of San Francisco and decided to stay.

Naturally, I found it difficult to believe anything he was saying, at first. But Olve was an earnest man. I'd never known him to lie, and he seemed entirely in possession of his faculties. And then, well, he told me that his powers were weak here because most magic doesn't operate well in our world. Nonetheless, he was able to do a small thing, there on the beach. He took a handful of sand and murmured over it—and as I watched, it fused into a glass heart. I wear it still, on a pendant around my neck.

How could I doubt him after that?

I asked him once if he could bring me to his world for a visit. But few beings can cross that barrier. Wizards and trolls are among them, and since I am neither of those things, I had to remain here.

Although my Olve remained in our world, he used his abilities to peek in at activities in his original home. Sometimes he would pop over to deal with some matter. He rarely divulged much about these missions, and I was fine with that. My own world was complicated enough.

After one of these expeditions, he returned home with you, Alfie—in doll form, of course, because he wasn't able to transport you otherwise. He told me that you had been in extreme distress and the only way he could save you was to bring you here. For some years afterward he tried to restore you to your true form, but he failed. It quite plagued him.

And then one afternoon he traveled to his home world—and never returned. To this day I don't know what happened. I thought perhaps he was killed trying to save someone else. I married again eventually—twice, in fact—but never stopped missing him.

In any case, life does go on. But one more odd thing happened. Thirty years ago, the Count and I were enjoying a glorious spring at his ancestral castle. We had so many wonderful parties there, with all the most delicious food and wine, and everyone dressed in the latest fashions, and views across the terraces to the mountains.

It was very late one night after one of our parties. The guests had all gone home or, for those staying with us, had gone to sleep. Though the Count was in bed, I was restless and roamed the halls. When I wandered into the conservatory, I found a woven basket, and inside that basket was a large baby—with remarkably bushy hair—staring at me solemnly. A note was pinned to his blanket, and although the handwriting was scrawled as if the author had been in a great hurry, I thought perhaps it looked a bit familiar.

Although I long ago lost the note, I remember it well: *Abandoned by parents after battle. Nobody to care for him. I can't—and can't return. Please find him safe home.*

I knew this child was a troll. Olve had described them, you see, and as I said, only a select group of beings can cross worlds. I also knew from Olve that trolls had a terrible reputation. But this was a baby who had no one. How could I fail him?

Coincidentally, or perhaps nothing is truly coincidence, my goddaughter Isabella had been seeking to adopt a child. She'd been unsuccessful in this regard because she wasn't married. I told her everything I knew about this baby. She flew to Italy and from the moment she set eyes on him, she loved him. "He deserves a family," she said. "He will grow up to be a fine man."

And she was right.

THIRTEEN

"She took me in despite knowing what I am?" Tobias knew the answer but needed to hear it.

"She took you in *because* she knew what you were: a child who needed a parent."

His heart felt lighter hearing this. He hadn't been an unwanted burden, and his identity hadn't been an obstacle. "Do you think it was Olve who brought me to you?"

"I honestly don't know. But I like to think that was the case. It's certainly something he would do."

It had been only a day since he realized he was a troll, and he hadn't yet had time to come to terms with all of the ways that might be significant. It only just now occurred to him that he must have been born in Alfie's world rather than this one. It was an odd thing to consider, but in a way it was also reassuring. It helped explain why he'd always felt out of place. He was literally an outsider.

Alfie, who had been subdued since Aunt Virginia scolded him, spoke softly. "Your family must have been from the Kingdom of the Twisted River. It's adjacent to Snjokarl's kingdom and has a small troll population. They often get into skirmishes with the other beings in their region."

Tobias wondered whether the trolls were entirely to blame for those conflicts. Alfie would probably assume so. Tobias also wondered vaguely about the circumstances of his abandonment. Were his biological parents dead? Did they survive but find themselves unable to care for a baby in the midst of battle? Were they separated from him by accident? He didn't feel any emotional connection to them, just a deep gratitude that he'd ended up somewhere safe and loving.

"Aunt Virginia, can I ask you another question? How come you gave Alfie to me?" He winced a little at his phrasing, but he couldn't think of a better way to say it. Alfie seemed interested in the issue, cocking his head slightly as they waited for her to respond.

She gave a small shrug. "If you're asking whether I knew you could restore him, I did not. I didn't think it was a possibility after Olve had failed, especially since you are not a wizard. But I am very old, and I wanted to ensure that the doll—that Alfie—was well cared for. And I knew, Tobias, that you could be trusted with this. I do apologize for the responsibility I saddled you with. I hadn't expected the onus to be so heavy."

"I don't mind. It feels good to be useful."

Alfie stood and bowed to Aunt Virginia. "I thank

you for your stewardship, my lady. I am greatly in your debt."

"I did nothing but stow you away in closets for decades. Tobias is the one you should be thanking."

After a brief hesitation, Alfie bowed to Tobias as well, and Tobias responded with what he hoped was a regal nod. He didn't really want acknowledgment, especially from Alfie. But he wasn't about to act rudely in front of the Countess of Contovello.

Anyway, there were bigger fish to fry. As Alfie retook his seat, Tobias turned to her. "You've filled in a lot of the blanks for us. But this bad guy named Snjokarl has been sending troll thugs after Alfie. Do you know how we can protect him?"

She frowned thoughtfully. "You might be able to transfer him home, Toby. More elegantly than my Olve did, I believe. My understanding is that this would be within your capabilities. You would have to accompany him, but then you could return here immediately if you chose to do so."

Alfie nodded. "Yes. This is what you must do. Then they will leave you alone."

"But they won't leave *you* alone, will they? If I drop you off, they'll...." He let the rest remain unspoken.

Alfie opened his mouth to respond, but Aunt Virginia stopped him with a raised hand. "Alfred, have you anyone at home you may turn to for assistance or protection?"

"No," he said grimly. "I have nobody."

And there it was. He had managed to make Tobias

fall in love with him and then had broken Tobias's heart, all in the space of a few days. But that hadn't really been Alfie's fault. Now he was all alone in not one world but two.

A chunk of knowledge struck Tobias so hard and so suddenly that he initially thought they were experiencing an earthquake and the building was falling down. The ground, however, was steady—it was Tobias himself who was shaken.

He stood up slowly and crossed his arms. "I know what to do."

FOURTEEN

"Absolutely not."

That was Alfie speaking, although Aunt Virginia had said pretty much the same thing. Tobias had outlined his plan and the two of them had instantly vetoed it.

Except he was a grown man, dammit—grown troll, whatever—and capable of making his own decisions. Neither of them could stop him. And neither had any alternative suggestions. Unless you counted Alfie's demand that Tobias dump him in Snjokarl's lap and then skedaddle back to his bungalow, his laptop, and his nuked Trader Joe's meals.

"I'm going," Tobias said stubbornly. "I won't drag you with me against your will, Alfie, but if I need to, I'll go alone."

"You'll be killed—or worse! I told you what Snjokarl is like, and he has a host of trolls to help him.

They guard him always. You can't beat him by yourself, and I would be of little help."

Tobias knew all that. He was also aware, at some level, that his insistence was foolish. But he also knew that if he didn't at least try, he wouldn't be able to live with himself. He shrugged. "Today is a good day to die."

Aunt Virginia huffed, and Alfie said, "That's a terrible thing to say. You're young. You have so much life to live."

"I was quoting someone else. I don't really want to die. But I get the sentiment. And Aunt Virginia, you're the one who told me to stop locking myself away."

"I meant you should date, not go on suicide missions."

"It's not a—" Tobias rubbed his forehead instead of trying to finish the sentence.

"I don't understand your intentions," said Alfie. "You could be free of me and all the dangers I expose you to. Instead, you choose to singlehandedly confront a sadistic elf who has a large retinue of brutal guards and who will not be dissuaded from persecuting me."

Tobias twitched one shoulder. "That's a reasonable summary."

After a moment, Alfie stood and, light-footed, crossed to where Tobias sat. He spoke quietly. "Is this because you are a troll? Are you trying to prove that you're not beastly like the others?"

Tobias was more fatigued than angry. "I'm not trying

to prove anything. Look, I might not have known my true identity until today, but I *do* know I'm not a murderous asshole. My mother raised me better than that. In fact...."

He stood, which made Alfie retreat a few steps. Tobias wasn't trying to intimidate him, but he was going to make a little speech and felt he ought to do so on his feet instead of slouched in the torture chair.

"My mother marched for women's rights and gay rights. She volunteered with community organizations to mentor young people of color. When she saw injustice, she spoke up. She wrote letters, cornered politicians in their offices, donated money, posted signs, gave lectures.... She made her voice heard. And as a single parent, she took in a baby troll and made sure he always knew he was loved. She taught me that nobody should abuse their power, and that it was worth making personal sacrifices for important causes. She also taught me that if a battle is important enough, sometimes you need to fight it even if you know you're going to lose. Especially when nobody else is going to rise to the challenge."

For a moment, his little audience simply stared. Then Aunt Virginia stood, came to him, and wrapped him in a gardenia-scented embrace. "I am so proud of you, Toby. Your mother would be too."

He hugged her back—gently, because she felt frail —and they both sniffled a bit. Then she pinched his cheek and returned to her chair.

That left Alfie, standing like a statue of an elf in poorly fitting clothing, his eyes as bright as flames. He came closer to Tobias—and then dropped to his knees and bowed his head. "Please forgive me," he said, his gaze trained on the floor.

It took a moment for Tobias to recover enough to answer. "For what?"

"I have behaved abominably. Your behavior on my behalf has been nothing less than heroic—I acknowledged this myself—and I have distrusted you, maligned you. I have treated you poorly, Tobias, and for that I am deeply sorry."

"You've had terrible experiences with trolls. I'm a troll."

"And I have judged you by that rather than by your actions, which was a terrible thing to do. And I *knew* better! I saw your beauty from the very beginning, and yet I stupidly turned away from that."

Kneeling must be uncomfortable for a guy who was still recovering from torture. Tobias held out a hand and helped Alfie to his feet. "I think I'm a pretty decent person, but I'm not beautiful. You don't have to—"

"But you are!" Alfie grasped Tobias's hands with his own. "Don't you understand? Just as trolls have particular talents, so do elves. One of those is that when we look upon a person, we see past their skin and faces and bodies. We see their true selves. That is how we judge beauty. And you, Tobias, are gorgeous."

That wasn't an adjective Tobias had ever expected to be applied to him, but Alfie seemed sincere. Deciding that this was one of those situations where actions spoke louder than words, Tobias grabbed

Alfie's shoulders, bent a bit, and gave him a kiss. He wasn't sure whether Alfie wanted this, so it was a tentative kiss at first. Just the gentlest connection of lips. But Alfie immediately made a desperate sort of moan and threw himself into the activity wholeheartedly. As Tobias had noted before, he tasted like mint.

It was the type of kiss that made you momentarily forget that ill-behaved trolls were trying to kill you and that you were standing in the middle of your godmother's parlor. For a brief time, nothing in two worlds mattered except that kiss. It was monumental.

But kisses cannot go on forever, unfortunately. Alfie and Tobias separated, both of them breathless and wide-eyed. Aunt Virginia, meanwhile, was watching with an expression of satisfaction. "That, Toby, is the way to carpe your diem. Well done." She stood and brushed imaginary crumbs from her clothing.

"Sorry, Aunt Virginia. I'm being rude. I'll just—"

"You'll do nothing at this moment. You two are going to stay—no arguing, boy—where you'll be safe from attack."

Alfie argued for him, which was a nice change. "My lady, you are exceedingly generous. But we cannot stay here like caged birds."

"Nobody knows that better than I do. Sometimes a prison is mistaken for a refuge. But you can spend tonight, at least, and face your difficulties in the morning, refreshed. My spare bedroom hasn't been used in decades, and I haven't had the opportunity to entertain since... well, it's been far too long. Besides, it's the holidays. I will provide a festive meal for all of us today, the pair of you will get a nice night's sleep, and you'll be ready in the morning to conquer your demons."

While Tobias was set on facing Snjokarl, he wasn't in any hurry to do so this exact second. He'd experienced a series of trying days, and a little break would be nice. Besides, since this would likely be the last time he'd see Aunt Virginia, it would be nice to spend a little extra time with her.

"How can we help, my lady?" Alfie looked eager.

"Please get the spare room ready. You'll find cleaning supplies and fresh linens in the closet. Feel free to get some rest as well. I'm just going to change and then I'll go out for provisions." She clapped her hands. "I find myself so looking forward to a holiday meal!"

Tobias glanced outside, where the sun shone brightly. "Um... I could go pick up groceries."

"And risk getting attacked? I think not. I won't order a delivery either."

"But—"

"But I'm a recluse?" She smiled at him. "Yes, I honestly can't remember the last time I went out in daylight except to a doctor appointment. But that, my dear, is because I am a great fool. I'm still alive, and I ought to act like it. If you can face an evil elf, I can most certainly do a bit of shopping."

He thought he'd lost that cinnamon-roll feeling,

but now it came back. He'd inspired Aunt Virginia to be brave.

Alfie, however, looked concerned. "Will you be safe, my lady? The trolls—"

"They can't harm me. Nor you, as long as you stay within this apartment. And I must get moving before the day grows later. I estimate that my errands will take approximately two hours." She winked at Tobias before sweeping out of the room.

That meant Tobias and Alfie were alone, which was a bit awkward. A lot of emotions had passed between them today. Tobias knew what he *wanted* to do—grab Alfie and make out until they were unconscious from lack of oxygen—but he didn't know what he *ought* to do. Or what Alfie wanted.

Luckily Alfie saved him. "Shall we go prepare the room, as she suggested?" He smiled.

"Okay."

Tobias hadn't actually been in this room since he was a young boy. He and his mother used to sleep there during their visits—she on the bed and he in a nest of cushions and blankets on the floor. It had changed very little since then, with an ornate four-poster still dominating the space. There was also a shelf stuffed with books and a dresser that matched the bed. Although the furniture was made of dark wood, the room was far from gloomy, thanks to the large windows with views of the bay. One of the windows had a built-in seat, and as a child Tobias had loved sitting there and watching the activity on land and water below.

"The photos are of you." Alfie turned slowly as he took in the decorations on the walls.

"And Mom, yeah." School pictures of each of them from every year, along with high school and university graduation shots. But also a few photos of the two of them together—at the beach, at Disneyland, in the desert—with Mom looking radiant. None of it had the feeling of a shrine, but he had the sense that these photos were important to Aunt Virginia.

"Your mother was stunning. Such a beautiful family!"

They were, weren't they? Tobias had thought he lacked Alfie's elfin skills to see inner beauty, but it turned out that wasn't true.

As promised, the closet contained a set of lavender-scented sheets, along with a broom and dustpan, a dusting cloth, and a few other odds and ends. More than enough, since aside from a bedding change, the room didn't need more than a quick tidy. Tobias wondered whether Aunt Virginia had a maid service or managed the cleaning herself.

"Oh, look at that!" exclaimed Alfie, pointing at a large box made of clear plastic.

"Holiday decorations. Aunt Virginia used to let me put them out."

Alfie's eyes sparkled. "Do you think she'd mind if we did that now? I don't want to upset her, but some holiday cheer wouldn't go amiss."

No, Tobias decided, it wouldn't. "Why don't you go

decorate the dining room while I tackle this room? There's not much to do in here."

In answer, Alfie danced close, tugged Tobias down for a kiss on the cheek, and then grabbed the box and danced away. The entire time that Tobias swept, dusted, and made the bed, his skin tingled where Alfie had touched him.

His task was soon complete, and when he went to check on Alfie, Tobias gasped at what he found. In a short time period and with only a box of simple ornaments, Alfie had transformed the dining room into a holiday marvel. Glass ornaments in gold, silver, red, and green hung from the chandelier and were scattered artfully on the large table. Artificial tree boughs that looked real were twisted around the curtain rods, helping to frame another lovely bay view. Electric candles flickered on the tabletop, the sideboard, and the windowsills. And in the center of the table, several small porcelain elves were perched on skis with wrapped gifts in their hands.

"Not bad, yes?" Alfie looked very pleased with himself.

Tobias pointed at the elves. "They're not enchanted too, are they?"

"I don't believe so. They say *Made in China* on the bottom."

That was a relief. Tobias was thrilled to have met Alfie, but a single elf had certainly brought a sleighful of problems. He didn't want to think what half a dozen could do. Besides, he couldn't wish from the bottom of his heart for all of them to be real.

"When will the countess return?" Alfie asked. There was a certain sparkle in his eyes.

Tobias glanced at his watch. "Hour and a half, I guess."

"Time enough."

"For wha—"

Before Tobias could complete the question, Alfie had grabbed his hand and was dragging him toward the bedroom. He was fairly strong. But Tobias was a lot bigger and hadn't been tortured or turned into a doll, so in theory he could have resisted.

He didn't.

As soon as they were inside the spare room, Alfie shoved the door closed and threw himself into Tobias's arms. It felt wonderful to Tobias, just holding him, feeling his solid body and the warm tickle of his breath. His pointed ears flushed rose-pink.

"I behaved like an ass and treated you atrociously. If you are too angry or hurt to want me, I understand. I'll—"

Tobias kissed him.

Yes, he had been upset, but he also understood why Alfie had behaved as he had, and Alfie had admitted he was wrong and apologized. Tobias wasn't prone to holding grudges. And he felt deeply for this creature who had brought literal magic into his mundane life and had helped him understand himself. Not just the part about being a troll, but the rest as well. Because of

Alfie, Tobias considered himself brave and capable and, well, heroic.

Also, Alfie felt lovely and smelled like candy.

Tobias would have guessed that making out with Alfie would be a bit uncomfortable due to their height difference, but bending down a little was no hardship, and Alfie sort of half climbed him anyway.

"May I undress you?" Alfie panted.

"Gods, yes, please."

"I'm afraid we shall have to be rather rushed due to the countess's imminent return. Which is a shame—I should prefer to savor you. But I doubt I'd last long anyway. You overwhelm me, Tobias."

Fast, slow... Tobias was eager for Alfie any way he could have him. But he stopped Alfie's roaming hands for a moment. "Are you sure you feel up to it? You're injured."

"The only pain I feel now is the burning of my desire."

Tobias, who wasn't capable of matching Alfie's fancy talk, decided that actions spoke louder than words. Laughing, he scooped Alfie into his arms, carried him across the room as if he were a bride, and set him down on the newly made bed. Alfie gazed up at him, seemingly delighted. "A man who takes charge! Delightful!"

"I'm not really...." Tobias felt himself blush.

"Tell me what you want from me, please. It would bring me great joy to give you exactly what you wish for."

That was a dizzying offer. "Well... you could start with more skin."

"Of course!"

As Tobias fumbled with his own buttons and zipper, Alfie stripped out of his clothing so quickly it *must* have been magic. And there he was, naked: pale and sleek and perfect despite the few lingering bruises and healing wound. His tattoos sparkled and spun hypnotically.

Tobias, on the other hand, was chunky and hairy and decidedly imperfect. But still Alfie stared at him bright-eyed and grinning, cock hard, one hand reaching for Tobias. If he was faking desire, well, he was a damned good actor.

"What next, my Tobias? Please tell me it involves touch. I so very much want to touch you."

Tobias responded by joining him on the bed.

A lot of touching happened after that—with fingers but also with lips and tongues. Tobias took care to avoid Alfie's sore spots, but that still left plenty of elf to explore, and of course Alfie had veritable acres of troll to play with. *Play* being the operative word, because while their connection was intense enough to make them gasp and moan, to make Tobias's blood roar through his body, it was also joyous and fun. They laughed together as each discovered delightful things about the other. Sex for Tobias was not only rare; it had also been destination-oriented. This time was all about the journey.

And what a journey it was!

By the time he and Alfie collapsed onto the mattress together, sweaty and sated, their time was nearly up. But neither was in a hurry to get up and dressed. Tobias liked the natural feel of Alfie snuggled against him, as if they'd been created to be together, as if they'd been doing this for years.

"Imagine," Alfie said after a gentle kiss to Tobias's shoulder. "If we are this good on our first try, imagine what we could manage with a bit of practice."

"We could win medals."

"I had thought I'd want to adventure with you, given the opportunity. And I would. But if we were granted more time, I'd want to spend much of it in bed with you. Making love, yes, but also talking. Simply *being*—together."

They sighed in unison, knowing it was nothing but a fantasy.

FIFTEEN

Aunt Virginia exclaimed happily over the decorations before leading Alfie and Tobias into the kitchen. "Much of our feast is precooked, I'm afraid. I've neither the time nor the endurance to make everything from scratch."

Tobias sniffed the air appreciatively. "It smells delicious."

"And I had such fun shopping for it all! It's foolish, really. I've spent so many years fearing that others would appraise me poorly now that I am no longer young and beautiful. But the world doesn't revolve around me, does it? Most people simply want to get on with their own day, their own business. And why should I care what strangers think anyway?"

"We know you're beautiful," Tobias said.

"Yes. Just as I know the same of you. And that is what is important." She rubbed her hands together. "If

145

you boys would set the table, I'll go get dressed for dinner."

Tobias looked down at his sweater and jeans. "We're not, uh—"

"You are both perfect." And she left the room.

When she returned fifteen minutes later, she wore a ruby-colored ballgown with a full skirt and sleeveless bodice. The glass heart pendant glittered at her neck. She smoothed the fabric of her dress. "I know I'm far too old to wear something like this, but—"

"You are a vision," said Alfie. "That color suits your complexion perfectly and the cut accentuates your elegant neck."

"The last time I wore this was to a New Year's Eve gala I attended with Olve. He wasn't usually much for big events, but he made an exception now and then, and he made quite a handsome picture in coat and tails. I wish I had a photo from that night, but at least I kept the dress."

Alfie bowed to her. "And you've generously shared this memory with us. Thank you."

Soon afterward they sat down for dinner. There was far too much food for three people, but everyone wanted a taste of everything and it was all mouthwatering. Roast pork loin, polenta, warm crusty rolls, cranberry chutney, root vegetables with a balsamic glaze, a green salad with walnuts and beets, and two bottles of pinot noir from a friend's Sonoma Coast winery.

Everyone got a little tipsy and ate more than was

wise. Aunt Virginia and Alfie each told wild stories from their youths, and both seemed entertained by Tobias's much tamer tales of life in Portland. "One of my neighbors rides a really tall bike," he said. "I don't know how he gets on and off it. And he wears a top hat." And "There's a cat a couple blocks away who sits on his front porch until pedestrians walk by, and he gets mad if people don't pet him." And "One booth at the nearby vintage shop specializes in old Lego sets and vintage building toys. Sometimes I spend way too much time there." Nothing earth-shaking about any of that, but they were important to him, and neither Aunt Virginia nor Alfie found what he had to say insignificant. He realized that, aside from the loneliness, he *liked* his life.

Dinner concluded with a sour-cherry trifle, forty-year-old port, a round of sincere toasts, and more laughter.

The evening was a true celebration, the first that Tobias had experienced since his mother died, and it was glorious. Not because the food was plentiful and delicious and the wine expensive, but because of the company. Tobias loved these people and was loved by them. It wasn't a large family, by any means, but it was a special one. A good one.

Eventually, however, Aunt Virginia stood. "I can't remember the last time I was so happily exhausted."

"We'll clean up," Tobias assured her.

She waved a hand. "It can wait until morning. If you boys could just put away the leftovers—oh, so many leftovers!—that will be enough. Unwashed dishes overnight are not the end of the world. You need your rest as well. And I'm sure you're desperate for some quiet time together." She winked broadly and left them. Tobias tried unsuccessfully to stop a blush.

As instructed, Tobias and Alfie put away the food. They rinsed the dishes and set the pots and pans to soak, mostly because Tobias hated a messy kitchen. It turned out that Alfie, due to his background, didn't really know his way around a kitchen, but he listened to Tobias's directions, made a good effort, and it all turned out well.

Then they were back in their borrowed room, standing together at the window, gazing out at the lights sparkling in the bay. "I have a heart's desire as well," Alfie said eventually, his voice almost a whisper. "Something I'd wish for if I performed the ritual that you did."

"I could maybe find you some edibles and Lego if you want to do that." He'd have to google to see what was open at this hour.

Alfie looked up at him with a sweet smile. "No thank you. I'm speaking hypothetically. It would all be a waste anyway, given what's going to happen to me soon."

That big dinner suddenly felt heavy in Tobias's stomach. "Maybe it won't happen. Maybe we'll figure something out."

"Perhaps," Alfie said, but without any conviction. "In any case, I am exceedingly grateful to have had the opportunity to meet you—although I'd feel happier about it if I wasn't leading you to your doom."

"You're not leading me anywhere. It's my choice." Tobias decided to change the subject. "What would you wish for?"

"Family."

"Oh."

"It wasn't until tonight that I fully realized how badly I want that. Once upon a time I had a father and an older brother, but now.... Tonight, with you and the countess, that was as close to perfection as I could ever dream of. I would desire more of that."

Tobias blinked a few times. Perfection. It had been a single dinner with a wounded elf, an eccentric old lady, and a data-engineer troll. Not a feast in a palace. Not zillions of siblings and cousins and nieces and nephews.

But it had been pretty close to perfect, hadn't it?

"We should get some sleep," Tobias said.

"Well, we should go to bed, at any rate."

Tobias's entire body flushed—with desire rather than embarrassment—and he grew hard so fast that he felt a little dizzy. Carpe diem, right? They might be destined for disaster tomorrow, but they could damned well enjoy themselves tonight.

He stripped faster than he ever had and Alfie did the same, and this time they stood for several minutes, their eyes doing all the caressing. Alfie's bruises had faded to a pale yellow and his leg wound, no longer bandaged, now showed healthy-looking scar tissue.

His hair was somehow perfect despite all their adventures, he had no hint of stubble, and even though his eyes were an icy blue, they were as warm as a summer afternoon. The tips of his ears and the tip of his erect cock were temptingly pink. And his smile spoke of mischief and joy... and love.

"I found my heart's desire," Tobias said. "That means there's hope for you too."

"Hope for us both."

They ended up snuggled together beneath the blankets, languidly stroking each other as if they had all the time in the world. Their breathing synchronized as if they were joined in song. And weren't they, in a way?

Tobias's mother had taught him long ago that although Solstice festivals varied in their specifics, they tended to share a common theme: light emerging from the darkness. The hope dawning—quite literally—as people emerge from the longest night. A celebration of having survived thus far and an optimism that now the world will slowly improve. The triumph of life over death.

In that case, the joining of his body with Alfie's wasn't simply a carnal act but also a holy one. A sacred rite.

"I love you," Tobias murmured into Alfie's ear.

"And I you. Whether I have a few hours to live or many decades, I shall love you to my last heartbeat."

"I'd prefer the many decades."

Alfie chuckled softly. "As would I. In true troll fashion, you have captured me, Tobias. I never want you to release me."

And there it was. Like an unexpected and wonderful gift discovered beneath a Christmas tree, the formerly tricky facets of the original plan resolved in Tobias's mind. He didn't know whether it was a good and viable plan or if it would bring success. But it *was* a plan, and that was something.

He wrapped Alfie in a tight embrace. "Release you? Never."

CHAPTER

SIXTEEN

The morning dawned slowly, the shy sun tentatively rising behind a veil of clouds above the East Bay. Tobias had been awake for some time already, and he'd crept into the kitchen to scrounge leftover bread and cold pork roast, which he carried to the bedroom for breakfast. He'd already eaten his share, but Alfie still slept, his inhumanly long eyelashes fanned across his cheeks, his lips curled into a small smile.

There was really no hurry to get on with things. Aunt Virginia said they were safe here. But they couldn't keep themselves caged forever, and the longer they stayed, the harder it would be to go.

Besides, if Tobias was honest with himself, there was a certain part of him—likely the very trollish part —that itched for a fight. He wanted to confront Snjokarl, tell him what a fuckwad he was, and do his best to kick his ass. He could almost feel his hands connecting with flesh and hear the broken cries of his prey. And this morning, these feelings didn't even scare him. He would embrace these aspects of his psyche and try to use them for good.

He thought about the previous day, which had been a roller coaster for sure. But it had ended with the best holiday celebration he'd experienced in years, followed by the best lovemaking he'd experienced *ever*.

"It's a lovely view."

Tobias turned to see Alfie sprawled in bed, ogling him.

"Can I ask you something?" Tobias said.

"Anything."

"You said that trolls are, um, disagreeable loners. But they reproduce, right? I mean, here I am. Does that mean they have families?"

Alfie sat up, yawned and stretched, and gave a nod. "I'm no expert on the matter. But my understanding is that most trolls do find mates and that they are loyal to their mates and protective of their children. I don't know if they experience love the way that humans and elves do, but on reflection, I have no reason to assume that they don't."

"All right."

After a pause, Alfie got out of bed, padded naked across the floor, and placed his hands on Tobias's chest. "You know you're capable of love. You loved your mother, didn't you?"

"Yes," Tobias whispered.

"It seems to me that adults, regardless of species, should be able to decide for themselves how they want to be. Perhaps we are limited in some aspects—I can't cross between worlds on my own, for example—but that still leaves us much leeway. I can decide not to be a spoiled, judgmental ass. You can decide to be a family man, if it pleases you."

"It does."

Alfie stroked Tobias's cheek. "Then we shall consider ourselves family, even if our time is short."

Tobias sniffled a little but didn't cry.

Eventually Alfie ate his breakfast and got dressed, and they emerged together from their room. Aunt Virginia sat in the parlor, dressed in jeans and an elegant cream-colored sweater, her white hair held back with a golden headband, a book in her hands. She'd opened the curtains wide and set potted plants on the windowsills. "I hope you spent a good night," she said. She didn't bother to suppress the sparkle in her eyes.

Alfie bowed to her and Tobias dipped his head in greeting. He only blushed a little. "Thank you for such a good evening, Aunt Virginia."

"I should thank you. I haven't felt this alive in many years."

Tobias carried their breakfast dishes through to the kitchen, where he washed and dried them—along with the dishes and pans from the previous night's feast— and put everything away. It was a satisfying exercise.

When he returned to the parlor, Alfie and Aunt Virginia paused their conversation about books.

"I should have helped," Alfie said. "I apologize. Princes rarely engage in household chores, but if I survive, I'll do my best to remedy that."

"I don't mind. I like cleaning."

As they stood there, Tobias knew it was time to go. But he couldn't quite bring himself to pull the trigger. The corners of Alfie's mouth twitched and he turned to Aunt Virginia.

"My lady, I wonder if you could grant me one more favor?"

"Of course, darling."

"I don't know how these things are done here, but among my people...." He shifted his feet and cleared his throat. "When two people wish to cement their union, they pledge to each other before a beloved relative or friend. Assuming that Tobias is willing, would you be our witness?"

"I'm willing!" Tobias shouted, in case anybody had doubts. It didn't matter that he'd just met Alfie—or that they might be doomed. Thinking about marrying him made his heart sing.

Beaming, Aunt Virginia set down her book and stood. "Nothing would delight me more. But perhaps I should change to more formal clothing...." She smoothed a hand over her jeans.

"If you like, but not on my account, please. You are beautiful just as you are. Tobias?"

"You're perfect, Aunt Virginia."

"Well. In that case...." She looked regal as she gestured for them to proceed.

Tobias felt big and awkward, with no clue what he was supposed to do, but he was at least grateful that nobody had tried to stuff him into a suit. And then Alfie calmed him with a brilliant smile and a gentle hand on Tobias's arm. "It's considered good luck to cement a union during solstice seasons because they symbolize new beginnings. The couple will often renew their promises during the next equinox to signify balance and equality in their partnership. I am hopeful that somehow, three months from now, we'll be able to do exactly that."

"I hope so too," said Tobias.

Alfie took Tobias's big hands in his elegant ones. "With the Countess of Contovello as witness, I, Alfred Clausen, son of Claus Clausen, pledge to you my devotion, my loyalty, my respect, and my care. I cannot promise I will be faultless, but I do promise that I will do my best to be the partner you deserve. I promise to love you."

Tobias had to clear his throat a couple of times before he could speak, but that was okay. It gave him a little time to think. "With Aunt Virginia as witness, I, Tobias Hilmar Lykke, son of Isabella Lykke, pledge to you my honesty, my protection, my respect, and my loyalty. I'll be clumsy and weird a lot of the time, but I promise to do my best to be the partner that you deserve. I promise to love you."

There. Life-changing, but not so hard.

Alfie looked at Aunt Virginia expectantly and she nodded. "I, Virginia Segreti, Countess of Contovello, witness these pledges. I place upon this union all the blessings I can bestow. Alfie, welcome to our strange little family."

All three of them were teary-eyed as they did a group hug. Aunt Virginia exchanged cheek kisses with both of them, and then they all hugged again. Alfie and Tobias followed up with an enthusiastic kiss—on the lips, not the cheek—that seriously came close to making Tobias swoon.

He could have sworn that for a brief moment he felt a sparkly sensation all over his skin, as if champagne bubbles were popping. Could be magic. Or maybe it was simply delight that he'd just married the elf of his dreams.

But they couldn't bask in this bliss forever. "A honeymoon would be nice," Tobias said with a sigh. "But I think we'll have to settle for a trip to Snjokarl's palace."

Alfie's expression turned grim. "I wish we could at least bring weapons, but most don't travel well across worlds. Which I suppose is just as well, or else Snjokarl would have imported guns from your world long ago, and that would have been horrific. But still."

"We can improvise. Like we did with my statue. Remember the wrestling Greeks, Aunt Virginia? We used them to defend ourselves from attacking trolls."

"That seems apt," she said. "I am positive you boys will find a way to triumph."

Tobias wasn't quite as optimistic as that, but he'd give it his all. He looked at Alfie and asked the most important question. "Do you trust me?"

Alfie answered at once. "Completely."

"Good. Aunt Virginia, do you have some heavy rope somewhere?"

CHAPTER

SEVENTEEN

Aunt Virginia didn't have rope, exactly. But she did have drapery tie-back cords, which made an excellent substitute and looked impressive when knotted around Alfie's wrists. They were strong, too, and it would have been impossible for Alfie to escape if Tobias had used regular knots. However, for a short period in his early teens, Tobias had been fascinated by stage magic—which might have been an early clue about his origins—and had learned escape knots. They appeared sturdy enough but could be easily loosened with well-placed tugs.

Once Alfie was bound, Tobias made a few showy tears to Alfie's clothing. Nothing that would expose too much skin, but enough to give the impression that Alfie had been in a scuffle. He also messed up that soft blond hair.

"You could clout me a couple of times," Alfie suggested. "Give me a black eye and a split lip."

"I will *not*!"

"It would add to the realism."

"Don't care. I'm already going to have to drag you around and treat you like shit. That's bad enough."

Alfie shrugged and dropped the subject.

The longer they stayed, the harder it was going to be to leave. Tobias settled a hand on Alfie's shoulder, Alfie looked up at him with a brave smile... and Tobias realized he had no clue what to do next. "How do I actually leave?"

"I don't know. I can't do it myself, and when the wizard transferred me I was not aware of my surroundings."

Great. It wouldn't do much good to Google it, Tobias guessed, and Aunt Virginia didn't appear able to add any advice. However, he'd figured out the tracking thing on his own, so maybe he could do the same now.

As he had done in the mountains, Tobias cleared his mind and pictured a computer screen. It was blank until two windows appeared. They didn't contain anything at first, but within a few moments one screen showed Aunt Virginia's parlor with three figures standing inside. It was lo-res, like game graphics from the 80s, but the figures were recognizable as Tobias, Alfie, and Aunt Virginia.

The other screen, fuzzy at first, clarified slightly to reveal a wide hallway with stone walls—the type of hallway one might find in a palace, he supposed. He'd never been in a palace before, although he'd seen them on TV and in movies. This screen contained four figures, all of them bulky like Tobias. Trolls, presumably.

What he needed to do was move himself and Alfie from one window to the other. If life were computer programs and people were data, he'd accomplish this by cutting and pasting. So in his mind's eye, he highlighted his figure and Alfie's. Before he took the next step, he smiled at Aunt Virginia and squeezed Alfie's shoulder. "Ready?"

"I suppose I am."

"Hang on."

Tobias imagined typing Control+X.

The ground fell out beneath them, sickeningly, like one of those drop-tower rides at an amusement park. Alfie yelped, but Tobias managed to maintain a grip on his shoulder. Aside from the two of them, there was... nothing. No light, no sounds, no sensations. They could have been in a vast starless sky or deep in a bottomless pit. It was cold and terrifying— far worse that the prospect of fighting trolls and elves.

So Tobias focused again, this time mentally typing Control+V.

He and Alfie landed with a thump onto a stone floor.

Alfie collapsed at once, moaning, and Tobias didn't know whether he was truly hurt or putting on a show for anyone watching. In any case, at least he hadn't turned into a doll. Tobias kept his feet, not at all disoriented or unsteady. In fact, something about the atmosphere embraced him, making him feel instantly at home.

Several very large people ran at him, their faces set in grimaces and their hands clutching knives. Tobias stood firm, straddling Alfie's huddled form. It took absolutely no effort to snarl possessively. "He's mine!" Tobias growled.

The trolls skidded to a halt, but they didn't sheathe their weapons. It was weird to be surrounded by so many people his own size. But even though his heart thudded, he wasn't afraid. A part of him was cheering, was hoping he'd have the opportunity to hit these thugs, to kick them, to tear at their flesh with his fingernails, to bite—

Okay. That part of him really needed to chill out a bit.

"Who are you?" shouted the biggest troll, taller and heavier than Tobias. With his leather pants and tunic, as well as a giant snarl of hair that appeared to have never encountered a comb, he looked as if he belonged to a medieval motorcycle gang. Tobias could smell his breath from several feet away.

"I am Tobias." A single name felt like the way to go here, like Pink or Cher.

"We don't know you."

Tobias went with the absolute truth. "I'm from the Kingdom of the Twisted River. I've transferred Prince Alfred back from the other world, and I intend to present him to Snjokarl. I suggest you get out of my fucking way." The swear word was a nice touch, he thought.

The trolls ratcheted down their antagonism a notch or two. "We'll take him," the biggest one said.

"The hell you will. He's mine!"

Tobias had never felt possessive over anyone before. Truth be told, he hadn't really had a chance. But now that he was married to someone he loved, Tobias felt like a dragon guarding his hoard of gold. Trolls were, he suspected, not great at sharing. No wonder his mother had spent so much time emphasizing the importance of letting others play with his favorite toys.

For his part, Alfie still hadn't moved, which was worrying but also probably a good thing. This way the trolls kept their focus on Tobias.

He watched as they exchanged glances. It occurred to him that they might not be used to having anyone oppose them. They seemed uncertain how to react, and he decided to use this to his advantage. "Take me to your leader!" he roared with a crazed grin. He'd always wanted to say that.

After a moment, the head troll mumbled something that sounded like agreement. Tobias bent and hauled Alfie to his feet, trying to appear rough but actually be gentle about it. He wished he could comfort Alfie, who stood with head bowed and shoulders tense, shaking slightly. Being inside these walls again must be terrifying.

The trolls surrounded Tobias and Alfie, two in front and two behind, but whenever one of them got too close, Tobias growled and they moved away. It was a long hallway with ceilings barely high enough for trolls. Everything was made of heavy stone blocks except for the raw timbers that provided some support overhead and the wooden doors that appeared at random intervals. There were no windows or discernible sources of light, yet everything sort of glowed.

After a few twists and turns, the parties clomped up a long flight of uneven stairs, through a set of huge double doors, and into a much nicer area. Here the floors had carpet runners, and the walls were plastered and hung with framed paintings—landscapes mostly, but also portraits of elves who, despite their Christmassy-looking clothing, seemed more grouchy than festive. All of them, essentially, grinches.

They hadn't passed anyone on the lower level, but on this floor elves scurried around, avoiding eye contact with the trolls. None of them made any effort to help Alfie, who was flagging: stumbling over the carpets and breathing heavily. Tobias had to grasp his arm and drag him along. He hoped that he wasn't causing additional pain.

At long last they went up another flight of stairs and down another broad corridor, stopping at a single ornately carved door guarded by an officious-looking sentry troll. "His Highness is busy," she said. She slightly reminded Tobias of one of the concierges at Aunt Virginia's building.

The biggest troll huffed at her. "He'll want to know this. Tell him that the prisoner has been returned."

Her eyes widened, and for the first time she noticed Alfie, hidden behind bigger bodies. Then her face took on a calculating expression. "I'll take the prisoner to him." She reached out a hand.

Tobias twisted so that he blocked her access to Alfie. "No. He's mine."

She glanced at the quartet of goons as if expecting help, but in Tobias's estimation, they looked a little smug, as if pleased that someone else was having to deal with the rude newcomer. So she shrugged and stepped back. "His Highness is still awfully angry that *somebody* let the prisoner escape."

"Nobody *let* him escape," said the big guy. "It was that wizard's fault. And you know what happened to *him*." All of the trolls laughed nastily, as Alfie stiffened and Tobias's stomach clenched. What had Snjokarl done to Olve?

Before Tobias could think of a way to ask, Alfie spoke up. "Listen to you. Have you no pride or dignity? You follow Snjokarl blindly. You choose to be nothing more than vile murderers when you could be so much better."

"We haven't murdered anyone," protested a troll with poorly braided red hair.

"And what do you suppose your master will do to me?"

The redhead shrugged. "More torture, I guess. Like

with the wizard. Although honestly, I think death is better."

Did that mean Olve was still alive? If so, how long had he been suffering in Snjokarl's clutches? Tobias was shaky on the relationship between timelines in the two worlds.

It appeared that these trolls were prepared to argue with Alfie all day. Maybe they were procrastinating on presenting him to Snjokarl. Tobias took a few deep breaths, channeled all the fierceness he'd kept locked down for his entire life, and roared. "Take me to your goddamn leader!"

To his immense gratification, all five trolls fell back a step or two. The biggest one looked at the sentry and huffed, "They're all yours," then turned on his heel and marched off, followed by his buddies.

The sentry was not happy. "Follow me," she muttered. "And make sure that prisoner behaves himself."

"He's an elf, not a trained dog."

"He's a traitor and can't be trusted."

Defending Alfie wasn't wise right now, so Tobias kept his mouth shut. But if he managed to survive his meeting with Snjokarl, he'd make sure to set the record straight for this troll and everyone else.

She knocked on the door so hard that it rattled in the frame, then took a deep breath and swung it open.

"What?" came a peeved-sounding voice from inside.

"There's a troll here, Your Highness, and—"

"There are a *lot* of trolls here. The palace is infested with them."

"This one has brought you Prince Alfred."

"Bring him here!"

Alfie was shaking again, and Tobias had to drag him into the room. He felt rotten about it, which didn't improve his mood any. To the extent he'd considered it at all, he'd expected an evil lair filled with skulls and ropes and torture devices. Or maybe, since this guy was a prince, a room dripping with jewels and silks and golden everything. What he got was... an office. A large but not especially fancy one, with several bookshelves and cabinets and an immense wooden desk piled with papers and scrolls. The furniture looked old and well-used, the woven rugs were threadbare, and nothing hung on the walls. The two windows, unadorned by curtains, were streaked with dirt. Dust bunnies lurked in corners and cobwebs clung to the ceiling.

Several trolls also lurked in the corners, each of them armed with a heavy sword and looking as threatening as motionless beings could.

Snjokarl himself was unimpressive, standing beside the desk and wearing a neutral expression. Like Alfie, he was slender and delicately built, his hair tucked behind his pointed ears. He looked to be in his mid-twenties and was blandly handsome, although his lavender eyes were pretty. His tunic and hose were in muted browns and grays.

"You're not one of mine," he said to Tobias.

"I'm from the Kingdom of the Twisted River."

"Hmm." Snjokarl tilted his head quizzically. "How did you get him into your possession?"

"I found him. Heard you were searching for him." Both of which were generally true statements.

"*Where* did you find him?"

Tobias was considering the best way to answer this, as well as the best way to get his hands on Snjokarl, who was well out of reach. Then Alfie spoke. "You are nothing but a coward who uses brutes to further your perversions. Let me go, you filthy bastard."

Snjokarl completely ignored Alfie. "Well, where was he? And what sort of reward were you expecting?"

Again, Tobias didn't know how to respond. "How much will you give me for him?"

"You're not thinking you can negotiate with me, are you?" Snjokarl sighed. "You cannot walk out of here with him—a hundred trolls will stop you if I tell them to. But I'd prefer to avoid needless conflict. Would you like me to employ you? That would be suitable reward." He waved a hand around, indicating all the guard trolls, as if they were a good example of the joys Tobias could expect.

Tobias hadn't come in search of a job offer, and especially not a shitty one. If he accepted, however, maybe he could track down what had happened to Olve. Except that while he was busy doing so, Alfie would be subjected to torture, and there was no way Tobias would stand for that.

He really should have spent a little more time on this plan. Well, he couldn't back out now.

"I want money," he rumbled. "A lot of it." He stomped closer to Snjokarl, who didn't look at all alarmed. All of the trolls, however, reacted by raising their swords and moving closer.

"Did Queen Carola send you? What does she want?"

"Nobody sent me," replied Tobias, who had no idea who Queen Carola was.

"Well, I don't believe you're in search of a monetary reward. I've never known a troll who cared much about wealth."

That was mildly interesting because Tobias himself didn't crave much money as long as he could live reasonably comfortably. But he'd always assumed he'd learned that attitude from his mother, who never had much interest in material goods. However, now wasn't the time for a nature/nurture debate. "I don't give a fuck what other trolls want. I want money."

"You intrigue me. Hand the prisoner over to my guards and you and I can have a chat."

The guards came closer and Tobias bared his teeth. "None of them are touching him."

"Look. This is all quite amusing, but I have work to do, and the prisoner needs to be returned to where he belongs. He and I have some catching up to do." Something glinted in Snjokarl's eyes, and it wasn't holiday cheer. Alfie shivered violently.

"Why do you want him so badly anyway?" Tobias demanded.

"What business is that of yours? I don't need a reason, other than the fact that possessing him pleases me."

Tobias wasn't experienced in understanding elf psyches. If a human had been acting exactly like this, however, Tobias would have concluded that the guy was dangerous as hell and not of sound mind. A psychopath, maybe. There was no real reason to assume that elves were any different in this regard. It was clear, in any case, that Tobias wouldn't be able to talk Snjokarl into abandoning Alfie.

And while Tobias was ruminating over this, the trolls inched closer. One word from their master and they'd undoubtedly attack. The only reason they hadn't already was that Snjokarl would be angry if Alfie got sliced and diced, thereby depriving him of his toy.

Snjokarl smirked.

Rage descended on Tobias so suddenly and so fiercely, that it was as if he'd leapt into a fire. He literally saw red. How *dare* this insufferable prick harm Tobias's beloved! And it wasn't just Snjokarl he was furious at. It was all of the trolls. And, for that matter, every human who'd ever said cruel words to him because he was big and awkward and different.

Tobias bellowed and launched himself at Snjokarl.

It felt *wonderful* to lay into that miserable excuse for an elf. To feel fists meet with flesh and to wrap hands around that scrawny neck. To listen to his choked cries and see him jerk fruitlessly as he tried to get away. His eyes widened with terror, and that was good too.

The other trolls came at Tobias with swords raised, and Tobias didn't even care. Let them kill him—at least he'd end Snjokarl first. He'd tear him to pieces. He'd gouge out his eyes and bite out his throat and—

"Stop!"

At the sound of Alfie's shout, Tobias froze, as did all the other trolls. Even Snjokarl stopped struggling. Alfie had unbound his hands and grabbed a letter opener off the desk. He stood straight-backed and regal, without any sign of fear. "All of you—sheathe your weapons and fall back, or my troll will destroy your master!"

After a moment's hesitation, the trolls obeyed. Tobias didn't blame them; it would have been hard to ignore Alfie's commanding tone.

"Tobias, let him breathe. But don't let him go."

Oh. Right. Tobias was still strangling an elf.

He loosened his grip enough for Snjokarl to take several huge gasps. "How dare you! I am a *prince* and you are nothing but—"

"Shut up," Alfie snapped. "I'm a prince too, remember? That didn't stop you from...." He shuddered and then regained his composure.

"The King of the Kingdom of Five Sisters has disowned you and declared you an outlaw," Snjokarl spat. "You are prince of nothing. *You* are nothing."

Alfie maintained a stoic expression, but when Tobias saw hurt flash in his eyes, he gave Snjokarl a good shake. He thought about continuing to strangle him—it was such a satisfying activity—but Alfie gave a slight movement of the head and Tobias reluctantly desisted.

"I could snap his neck," Tobias offered helpfully. "Or yank out his tongue. Or both."

Alfie walked closer and set a gentle hand on Tobias's back. "Is that really what you want to do?"

"Yes. No. I don't...." He remembered his mother's lessons and wondered what she would have advised him to do in this situation. Yes, Snjokarl was smaller and weaker, but he was hardly blameless, and he had a small army of trolls backing him up. Nonviolence was all well and good in principle, but did it always hold up in practice?

Alfie went up on his toes so he could whisper in his ear. "Can you transfer all three of us?"

Tobias opened his mouth to say that was a good idea and to ask where to—

And the doors burst open, a flood of armed trolls surging toward them.

Acting mostly on instinct, he mentally highlighted himself and the two elves, cut... and pasted.

CHAPTER

EIGHTEEN

Snjokarl took off running as soon as they arrived, but Alfie tackled him to the ground. When Tobias caught up with the two of them, he gently pushed Alfie to the side before sitting on Snjokarl's back. That would make him stay put for a bit.

"Where is this?" Alfie looked around.

That was an excellent question. Tobias hadn't had time to pay much attention to that aspect when he was transferring them.

It was nighttime and they were outside. The air was cold—although Tobias was, as usual, comfortable —and it was damp but not quite raining. They were on an expansive grass lawn with some tall trees scattered around, a street running in front, and a large brick building behind them.

"I recognize this place," said Tobias with a degree of relief. "It's a college near my house."

Beneath him, Snjokarl made a pained moan. Tobias rose but grabbed him before he could run off, keeping a tight grip on Snjokarl's arm.

"What have you done?" snarled Snjokarl.

Alfie brushed some debris off his clothing. "We've been transferred."

"It won't save either of you. My trolls will track you down."

Tobias realized that was probably true, and it meant that he couldn't simply let Snjokarl loose to make his own way in the wilds of Portland. And now, back in his own world, Tobias's taste for murder had faded, which didn't leave many options.

Alfie looked thoughtful, however. "We are prepared to negotiate."

"I won't negotiate with the likes of—"

"We could just kill you instead. Sure, your followers will find us, but that won't bring you back to life." Alfie finished his statement with a sunny smile. And when Snjokarl made sputtering noises but couldn't quite manage to say anything coherent, Alfie came a little closer. "How does it feel to be alone and scared and powerless, knowing you are completely at the mercy of someone not known to be merciful? It's not pleasant, is it?"

Snjokarl had no answer for that either.

Alfie took a few deep breaths and then looked past Snjokarl to Tobias. "What are your thoughts, beloved?"

Tobias paused to give Snjokarl a shake because he was making offended noises, apparently at the thought of an elf loving a troll. Then Tobias shrugged. "I'll kill him if you want. He probably deserves it. But if you have another idea, I'm fine with that. Do what you think is right."

A softness came to Alfie's eyes before he nodded and focused again on Snjokarl. "We'll return you to your palace—alive—and never step foot again in your kingdom or Kol's. Under two conditions."

"What?" Snjokarl demanded sourly.

"First, you pledge to cease persecuting me. Send nobody to search for me, and do not harm me, Tobias, or anyone we care about. Ever."

It seemed to Tobias like a reasonable requirement. Alfie wasn't asking Snjokarl to make up for the fact that he'd poisoned Kol against his brother, causing Alfie to lose everything. And he wasn't requesting compensation for being tortured.

Snjokarl scowled but didn't refuse. "What else?"

"You release the wizard Olve Lange to our custody —also permanently, and without any future repercussions to him."

If Tobias wasn't already in love with Alfie, that would have done the trick.

"Interesting," said Snjokarl. "And you will not be tempted to win back your noble status, your birthright, your fortune... your home?"

"I've found something more valuable than any of those things."

"What?"

"Love. Which is something you'll never have."

175

It was a good comeback, and one with which Tobias fully agreed. But this was a terrible honeymoon. He was getting tired of standing here in the damp grass instead of snuggling in a big bed with his husband, so he gave Snjokarl another shake in hopes of speeding up his response.

"Very well," Snjokarl said finally and with poor grace. "I shall be delighted to be rid of you for good. Rid of all of you. You've done nothing but cause me trouble."

"You agree to my terms?"

"Yes. You have my word."

Alfie nodded. "Tobias, you can let him go."

Although Tobias was somewhat disappointed he wouldn't get a chance to tear Snjokarl to pieces, he was also relieved he wouldn't have to. He released his grip—more violently than necessary, perhaps—and gave Snjokarl a little shove, although not enough to knock him over.

"Where's Olve?" demanded Alfie.

"His quarters are adjacent to where yours were."

"That's the lowest level of the palace, Tobias. Dungeons. Can you take us all there?"

Of course, Tobias had never been to the dungeons and had seen very little of the palace. But he concentrated, imagining that the computer screen in his head looked remarkably like one of those 3D house plans you could explore in online listings at Redfin and Zillow. Instead of a cute 1920s Craftsman bungalow with an excellent walk score, however, he pictured

Snjokarl's palace. And there on the lowest floor was a blinking red dot.

"I can see his location. Hang on." Tobias grabbed Snjokarl again and with his other hand laced his fingers through Alfie's. He did the routine that was already starting to feel familiar: highlight, cut, paste.

When he opened his eyes, they were in a dungeon. At least, he assumed it was.

The long corridor had a white floor, possibly marble, and smooth stone walls occasionally interrupted by metal doors. Although there was a general glow of illumination, there was no obvious light source. The far end of the hallway was a blank wall, while the nearer end contained another metal door, wider than the others. There was a faint odor of dampness, and no sounds other than the rustlings made by the three of them.

"He's in here," Tobias said confidently, pointing at the nearest door; unlike the others, it had a spiky symbol painted on it. He couldn't sense anything on the other side, but his tracking ability had led him directly to the threshold.

Alfie had gone paler than usual—this place must hold terrible memories—but he didn't back down. "That cell is magic-proof. That's why you couldn't transfer us straight inside."

It also explained, Tobias assumed, why a wizard hadn't managed to escape. How did you magic-proof a room? Was it some kind of insulation, like eggcrate foam used in sound booths? Or a lining, like lead used for x-ray protection? He'd ask about it later.

"Unlock the door," Alfie commanded Snjokarl.

"I don't have a key. I shall need to call a guard."

"Do it."

Tobias followed Snjokarl to the door at the end of the hallway and watched as he knocked a few times. "It is your master," he called. "Open this door at once."

He was obeyed promptly, and a pair of trolls stood in the doorway, gaping. "Your Highness! We were told you'd been kidnapped and—"

"Yes, yes. Now come unlock the wizard's chamber."

One remained in the doorway while the other entered the corridor, squeezing by Tobias. The look she cast at him wasn't friendly, and he wondered if there was any possibility he could ever have a nice chat with another troll and find out more about his birth species. It would be interesting to learn which of his quirks were troll things and which were... just him.

The troll hefted an impressively large key, worked the lock, and then pulled the door open. When Alfie hung back—who could blame him?—Tobias pushed forward to look inside.

It was a windowless space about ten feet square, with featureless white walls and floor. As in the hallway, there was a sourceless glow. The only furnishings were a toilet, a sink, and a stone bench. A man sat on the bench with his knees drawn to his chest, his back pressed into a corner. His head was deeply bowed, and all that Tobias could see was a matted mass of dark hair.

"Olve?" asked Tobias. "Olve Lange?"

The man's only reaction was to curl more tightly into himself. It was no wonder he wasn't reacting well —Tobias was a troll.

Tobias took a cautious step into the cell and tried again. "Um, I'm Tobias Lykke. I think you rescued me when I was a baby? The Countess—um, your wife, Virginia, is my godmother."

Now the man did look up, eyes wide. "No. It's a trick."

"No, it's not, I promise. Look, let's just step into the hallway—Alfie's there; you rescued him too—and I'll get us the hell out of here."

But Olve hid his face again. "Stop tormenting me," he whispered.

Maybe it would be better if Alfie lured him out. Tobias started to turn around—and something hit him hard on the back of the head.

CHAPTER
NINETEEN

Tobias's ears discerned a conversation before he could make his eyes focus or get the rest of his body to do anything useful.

"—sorry. I didn't.... I couldn't trust...."

"You're not to blame," said a second voice. Alfie. That was Alfie speaking, and just hearing him was a relief, although Tobias couldn't quite remember why. "I was the one who foolishly thought Snjokarl would keep his word."

Tobias growled slightly and felt a cool hand stroke his cheek. "Shh," said Alfie. "You should lie still."

Tobias didn't want to lie still. He wanted to plunge his fist into Snjokarl's chest and yank out his beating heart. He wanted to hear Snjokarl scream and watch the life fade in his eyes. He wanted—

Where the hell was he?

It took several minutes to corral his thoughts into anything coherent and get his bearings. He was lying on his back on a hard floor, his head pillowed in Alfie's lap, Alfie's fingers gently combing his hair. His head hurt, his stomach was queasy, and even the slightest movement made things worse. The light was too bright even through closed eyelids.

"Alfie?" he managed. "Where...?"

"We're in Olve's cell. You got bashed in the skull and probably have a concussion. Usually I'd be able to work some healing magic on you, but not here. I'm sorry. This is all my fault." Alfie sighed loudly.

"Are you all right?"

"I'm fine. After the troll knocked you out, she picked me up and threw me in the cell with you two and then closed the door."

Tobias allowed himself to sort through these words until he understood them. His brain was like a very bad car, stuck in first gear and with the engine misfiring. Eventually he got it. "You're a prisoner again!" he groaned.

"We all are. I'm sorry. It's all—"

"Stop it. This is Snjokarl's fault, not yours."

Alfie didn't answer, but he did sigh again.

Moving very slowly over a few minutes, Tobias managed to sit up without puking. He patted the back of his head. Even a gentle touch was painful, but he didn't feel any fresh or dried blood, which he figured was good news.

"Tobias, maybe you shouldn't be upright."

"I'm okay. Just give me a few."

Alfie respected his request, although he did settle a

steadying hand on Tobias's arm. After a bit more time passed, Tobias was finally able to open his eyes and blink away most of the fuzziness.

Olve was still huddled on the bench and looking miserable. He wore filthy rags and had a tatty blanket around his shoulders. He was almost skeletal, his face and chest mottled with bruises and scrapes, but he was also much younger than Tobias expected. Upon consideration, however, he realized that made sense. Aunt Virginia had been in her early twenties when she married Olve—and when Olve disappeared. Time obviously moved differently in the two worlds.

"I don't suppose I can transfer us all out of here?" Tobias asked.

Both Olve and Alfie shook their heads. "You can try if you like," said Alfie. "But the magic-proofing...."

"I get it." And he did. Yet he tried anyway, just in case. Nothing happened. It was frustrating. He'd gone his entire life unaware that he possessed this talent, but now that he'd used it a couple of times, it was a comfortable fit. Now, it was as if he'd broken in a particularly nice hoodie only to have it taken away.

Although moving wasn't fun, Tobias repositioned himself so he was leaning back against the wall. "Is he going to kill us?"

"Not right away. And I don't think he'll simply abandon us here to rot. He'll want to... play." Alfie shuddered and so did Olve.

"How long have you been here?" Tobias asked Olve.

"No idea. Sometimes it stays light for what feels

like months. Sometimes it stays dark. I... I've lost time."
Then he blinked a few times and his eyes grew more
focused. "You mentioned Virginia. Is she still...? It's
been so long." He seemed to hold his breath waiting for
an answer.

"She's elderly but still doing well."

"Has she.... Has her life been happy?"

Tobias gave a comforting smile. "It has. I know she
misses you—she speaks of you sometimes—but she's
had so many adventures."

For the first time, Olve looked a little less despon-
dent. "Good. She's a remarkable person. And from the
looks of things, she made sure you had a good family."

"She did. I couldn't have hoped for a better
mother."

"And how did you and Prince Alfred become
acquainted?"

They had nothing else to do, and storytelling
would distract all of them for a bit, so Tobias and Alfie
told their tales. It was good to see Olve perk up when
he learned how much good he had done for both of
them, and that they'd ended up in love. At the end,
though, he shook his head sadly. "You could have
killed Snjokarl and gone on with your lives instead of
getting stuck here with me."

Alfie looked offended. "Do you think we could
abandon you, knowing what you've done for us and
knowing how much you mean to the countess?"

"My apologies. You are both fine and honorable
men."

That was nice to hear, although it didn't solve any of their problems. "Olve, how did you end up here?" Tobias asked.

"My story isn't as happy as yours—although I suppose we all have the same ending."

Olve talked for a long time, and neither Tobias nor Alfie was inclined to stop him. For one thing, they had nothing else to do but listen, and for another, being entertained was better than wallowing in misery. Also, it had likely been ages since Olve had experienced the opportunity to speak with anyone who wasn't imprisoning or torturing him.

But Tobias's head ached and his attention wandered, so he mostly caught just the major events: Olve had heard of Alfie's fate and tried to help. His magic skills were moderate, which is why Alfie didn't quite transfer successfully and Olve couldn't un-doll him. Olve had returned to his home world in hopes of getting the trolls to abandon Snjokarl's cause, and also because he didn't want the trolls anywhere near his beloved wife. He'd discovered an orphaned baby troll, sent him where he knew Aunt Virginia would find him, and shortly afterward was captured. He'd remained here ever since, with no hope except death.

When he finished, they were all silent for a while. At Alfie's urging, Tobias lay back down with his head in Alfie's lap. They both refused Olve's offer to use what passed for his bed. Tobias drifted a bit, stomach rumbling, thinking about the dinner they'd shared with Aunt Virginia. This wasn't how he thought he'd spend his wedding night. But then, until recently he'd doubted he'd ever marry at all.

Alfie resumed combing Tobias's hair with his fingers, which felt lovely. He seemed pensive. Eventually, he spoke in a quiet voice. "I refuse to believe that this is the end for us."

"But Alfie," Olve began.

"Oh, I know. Good doesn't always triumph over evil. Not all stories have happy endings. Terrible things happen to even the best people in both of our worlds. But still. There must be *something*. We have all had so much magic and wonder in our lives—I can't believe it would all suddenly disappear."

Tobias appreciated Alfie's optimism but didn't share it. Sometimes things were just shitty, and there was no rhyme nor reason to it. Very few people led a truly charmed life.

"I'll fight anyone who tries to hurt either of you," he promised.

Olve gave a sad smile. "You did turn out magnificently, didn't you? Everyone says such terrible things about trolls, yet they overlook the fact that most trolls simply want to keep to themselves and mind their own business." He sighed. "But fighting will do nothing but get you hurt. There are so many of them."

"I'm going to get hurt anyway. Might as well make at least one or two of them sorry they messed with us."

He closed his eyes and, lulled by Alfie's fingers, drifted into sleep.

THE FLOOR WAS HARD, the lights too bright, and nobody brought food, which left the three of them hungry, desolate, and crammed into a small cell. At least water and a toilet were available, for which Tobias was grateful. His skull was still tender, but the nausea, dizziness, and fuzzy-headedness had subsided.

He knew that as unhappy as the situation was for him, it was worse for his companions, both of whom had been tortured here. And while Tobias had plenty of padding to sustain him for a while, Alfie was much thinner, and Olve was emaciated.

Olve and Alfie were good company, however. Olve was happy to share stories about Aunt Virginia, about his own adventures, and about how he'd found Tobias. They both taught him a lot about their world, and in turn, they asked about the world he'd lived in.

"I wish I could see this operate," said Olve, cradling Tobias's cell phone in one hand. Nobody had bothered to empty Tobias's pockets before locking him up, but the phone was useless. Either the battery was dead or Apple products didn't work here.

"It's due to the magic-proofing," Alfie said confidently.

"But cell phones aren't magic. They use electricity, microchips, radio waves.... It's all just physics."

"Perhaps magic is physics as well."

Olve perked up. "That's an interesting idea. We can't generally see electricity or radio waves, but various devices can channel them in different ways. Magic could exist as an unseen force that is used in some ways by wizards, in others by trolls.... I so wish I had the chance to explore this! I would set up experiments, you see...." He chewed his lip, his mind clearly zooming through the possibilities.

Tobias thought about the different types of software he might modify to help with those kinds of experiments. The data would be fascinating to analyze.

"I'd start by magic-proofing a room," Olve said thoughtfully. "Although I daresay I'd make it more comfortable than this one. Tobias, can a room be made impermeable to the forces that make a phone operate?"

"Sure. Anything that's dense enough will work. I've had clients that couldn't use wi-fi in their offices because of what was in the walls. They had to use hard-wired connections instead."

Both Olve and Alfie stared blankly, and then Olve returned to his thoughts. Tobias's poor brain was ticking along too. "Hey," he asked them, remembering his question from before he lost consciousness. "How does a room get magic-proofed?"

They looked at each other as if each expected the other to have an answer. But then Alfie simply shrugged. "It's not something I've ever had interest in doing. In our castle we primarily used healing magic, and why would anyone want to block that?"

Olve rubbed his chin. "My apprenticeship ended too early and I never learned that, or a great number of other things that would have proved useful. Such as how to successfully transfer an elf without transforming him into an inanimate object."

Alfie reached over and patted Olve's foot, clearly wanting to show that he held no grudge.

Tobias, however, frowned in thought. Apparently Snjokarl had magic-proofed only this cell and not the rest of the palace, since Tobias had been able to use his tracking and transferring skills in other areas. It implied that magic-proofing required a physical space, and perhaps a limited one at that. What if it really was the same as blocking radio waves?

Tobias stood and stared at the nearest wall.

Alfie stood too and put a hand on Tobias's back. "Beloved? Are you all right? Is your head—"

"I'm fine." That came out snippier than intended, so Tobias gave him an apologetic smile. "Just give me a minute, okay?"

"Of course." Alfie stepped back.

The wall was... unremarkable. It was made of stone, just like the rest of the palace. But unlike the white walls and floor in the fancy parts of the palace, those in the hallway where they'd first appeared and in the dungeon had been plain gray. Nobody cared whether their dungeon looked upscale. Maybe here, the white wall served a utilitarian purpose.

Tobias scratched at it, but nothing happened. For the first time in his life, he wished he had claws instead of ordinary fingernails.

Wait a minute. He was a twenty-first-century guy, not a fairytale monster. He didn't need claws.

He reached into his pocket and pulled out a black nylon case.

"What's that?" asked Alfie.

"A Leatherman multi-tool set." Tobias removed it from the case to demonstrate. "See? It has pliers, wire strippers, a screwdriver, a knife... nineteen tools in all. Aunt Virginia sent it to me two Christmases ago. She said she thought it might come in handy for me at work. I don't really deal with hardware stuff, but you never know. I use the bottle opener pretty often, actually. And I got in the habit of carrying it around."

Olve was beaming. "That sounds exactly like the type of thoughtful gift Virginia would bestow."

"But how come I still have it? And my cell phone? And...." He dug in his pockets. "And my wallet, my keys, and my ChapStick. Shouldn't the goons have taken this stuff away before locking me up?"

Alfie looked uncomfortable. "It's because you're a troll, my love."

"Huh?"

"They misjudged you—as I did myself. When people see trolls, they assume they're capable of little more than mindless brutality. Even other trolls might assume this, because that's the message they've heard for their entire lives."

Tobias pondered this for a moment. "So if I can't pound anyone into a pulp, they don't see me as a threat."

"If you'd possessed a larger blade, I'm sure they would have taken that. But they likely didn't recognize your... Leatherman, was it? I'm sorry their appraisal of you was so negative."

Tobias, who wasn't sorry at all, grinned. "People have been misjudging me for my entire life. For once, maybe that's worked in my favor." He opened the diamond-coated file and began to scrape at the wall.

Alfie came closer but was careful to not get in the way, and then Olve got off the bench and, on slightly tottery legs, came over to watch as well. At first nothing happened, but as Tobias pressed harder, the white coating started to wear away. It was a very thick, sort of rubbery paint, and when Tobias was able to get his fingernails under the edge of it, he peeled away a strip about the size of his arm.

There was another layer underneath it, a sickly green.

"May I see?" asked Olve.

When Tobias stepped aside, Olve reached out and touched the green spot—and drew his hand back with a hiss. "It stings."

Both Tobias and Alfie felt a very vague tingle on contact, but nothing painful. "It's repelling magic," said Olve, seemingly fascinated. "Magic is a more integral part of a wizard—even a poor one like me—than of a troll or elf. Tobias, I do believe you've discovered how they do it."

Alfie clapped Tobias on the back. "Well done!"

Tobias would have liked to bask in the praise, but

he felt discouraged. "I think all four walls, plus the floor and ceiling, are coated in this. It'd take me forever to get it all off. We don't have forever."

He scraped at the green stuff and it came off, but in tiny flakes. It was like when he'd bought his house and had intended to strip the paint off the original woodwork. He'd given up after half a day and just repainted everything. Which had been fine back then, but now his life, his husband's life, and the life of his godmother's husband hung in the balance.

"Perhaps if even some of it is removed, our magics will work," Olve suggested. He looked more hopeful than Tobias had seen him, and that was something—as long as Tobias didn't crush that hope.

"Let me work at it for a bit," said Alfie, gently prying the Leatherman from Tobias's fingers. "I don't think you're fully recovered from your head injury."

"I can—"

"Tobias. Let me."

In truth, Tobias's head still ached, so he nodded and returned to what was now his usual sitting spot against the wall. Olve resumed his place on the bench, huddled under his tattered blanket, and watched. Alfie, whistling something that sounded suspiciously like "Santa Baby," started scraping away.

He had been at it for only a few moments when there was a noise at the door.

"It's them!" Olve hissed urgently.

Alfie reacted with inhuman speed—although maybe it was normal elf speed. He tossed the

Leatherman to Tobias, who caught it and tucked it in a pocket as Alfie leaned back against the wall, hiding the peeled spot with his body.

The door heaved open and a particularly burly troll immediately blocked the opening. Tobias could just barely see two more trolls standing in the hall immediately behind him. "Traitors," growled the first one. He flung a bulky sack onto the floor, backed out, and slammed the door shut.

After a pause to make sure he wouldn't return, Tobias sagged with relief.

"That's food." Olve sounded distressed.

"Is there something wrong with it?" asked Tobias.

It was Alfie who answered. "They always feed you before he...." His throat made a choked sound. "He doesn't want you to faint too soon."

Okay, that was it. That. Was. Just. Fucking. It.

Tobias leapt to his feet, pulled out the Leatherman, and attacked the wall as if it were Snjokarl. He imagined scraping his blade over the smug, cruel face, tearing away the flesh until nothing was left but a pile of shattered bones. He knew this was awful imagery and probably frighteningly trollish, but at the moment he just didn't care. His mother had told him that physical activity was a healthy way of displacing anger, and oh *boy* did he have a lot of anger to displace.

He didn't know how long he worked—everything was just a red blur. But it felt like only a few minutes before he had scraped both white and green coatings away from a swath of wall almost as big as he was.

"Will magic work now?" he asked, probably too loudly. He probably looked terrifying. Olve seemed a little alarmed.

Alfie, on the other hand, was staring at him with shining eyes. "You are *stunning*, my love."

As serious as the situation was, Tobias couldn't quite suppress a pleased grin. Then, in a softer tone, he asked again, "Will it work now?"

"I'm not sure...." Olve chewed his lip. "I'm not that skilled to begin with, and—"

"Allow me," said Alfie. He put a gentle hand against the sore spot on Tobias's head and hummed.

This time Tobias was sure of the tune. "Mariah Carey?"

"Shh. Let me concentrate." Alfie resumed humming, and after a few seconds Tobias's scalp registered an agreeable tingle accompanied by a gentle warmth. He closed his eyes and had to bite back a moan of pleasure—not sexual, more like the kind emitted during a good stretch or a perfect massage. His headache faded, along with the dizziness and brain-fuzz.

Alfie gave Tobias's shoulder a quick kiss and stepped back. "It's working."

Olve muttered something that sounded like a prayer, and Tobias was tempted to join in. But they weren't free yet. "So what should we do? I can zap all three of us out of here."

"That will buy us some time." Alfie looked grave. "But it won't be a permanent solution."

Right. Snjokarl would have his minions track them down right away.

Tobias scratched the beard that was starting to grow and distractedly acknowledged that he really preferred to be clean-shaven. "So if Snjokarl was out of the picture, would his trolls still come after us?"

"Unlikely. Without him to boss them around, they'd just give up."

"What about your brother?"

"The trolls have no loyalty to him. And I doubt he'd bother pursuing any of us. He wanted me gone." Alfie gave a sad shrug.

So getting rid of Snjokarl was the solution. Honestly, Tobias had pretty much known that from the start. "Before, we were willing to just abandon him in the other world. But now I don't trust him enough for that. I'm afraid he'd figure out a way to get back here."

"I concur," said Alfie. Olve nodded in agreement.

"But as much as I want to tear him to tiny shreds— and I really, really do—I'm not sure I could live with myself if I committed cold-blooded murder."

Alfie embraced him. "We all have baser instincts. Unlike Snjokarl, you have the morals and strength of character to control yours."

"At the moment it would be handy if I didn't." Tobias was also aware that he didn't have time to be gloomy about it.

"There... might be another option," said Olve.

CHAPTER

TWENTY

A hasty plan was concocted.

It wasn't a good plan. They all agreed that it relied too heavily on assumptions and luck. But they didn't have time to come up with anything better. "And besides," said Alfie, "isn't this the season for miracles?"

Tobias patted his shoulder. "We're asking for a lot more than oil lasting for eight days."

So despite the misgivings, they went forward with it anyway.

To begin with, they ate. Sort of. The bag contained a hunk of moldy bread, a few mealy apple-like fruits, and several pieces of mystery meat. As awful as it was, it was more food than Olve had seen in a long time. At Tobias and Alfie's insistence, he consumed the bulk of it, promptly felt ill, and was just as promptly healed by Alfie. He left a few bites for each of them, and they managed to choke them down—more out of politeness than need—since neither of them had reached Olve's level of hunger.

Shortly afterward, the trolls barged in. Before they could hurl their first insult, Olve pointed a finger, mumbled something unintelligible, and froze them in place.

"That's impressive!" said Tobias, poking the nearest one pretty hard.

"It's a simple spell, and it won't last long. We should go."

They paused long enough for Tobias to make sure all three immobile trolls were fully inside the cell and for Alfie to take a knife and a set of keys from one of them. Locking the trolls inside the cell proved unexpectedly satisfying, especially after Alfie somehow managed to turn off the light inside.

"Are there any other prisoners?" Alfie asked Olve.

"I don't know."

They unlocked all the other cells, which were empty. None of them looked to be magic-proofed.

By the time they reached the end of the corridor and climbed the stairs, Olve was flagging. "Go on without me," he gasped, leaning against the wall.

"No," Alfie and Tobias replied in unison.

Alfie unlocked the door and, with Tobias tracking Snjokarl and half carrying Olve, they crept through the halls. The whole thing reminded Tobias of a scene in *The Princess Bride*—a movie he and his mother had loved to watch together—and he nearly broke into hysterical laughter. Alfie had to poke him a few times to keep him moving properly.

The few windows they passed showed darkness outside, and Tobias sensed it was pretty late. That likely explained why they didn't encounter many other people. The few they did bump into stopped in shock, and that gave Olve the opportunity to freeze them before they could scream for help.

They finally reached a door at the very end of a long, narrow hallway, guarded by a pair of sleepy-looking trolls who were immobilized before they knew what hit them. "Can't do much more," rasped Olve, who by now was literally draped in Tobias's arms. His face was even more drawn than usual. Clearly, magic took energy, and he hadn't had much to begin with.

Alfie gave him a reassuring pat. "No worries. We're nearly there." Then he took a deep breath and flung open the door.

It was a torture chamber. Not exactly like the ones Tobias had seen in movies—this one looked more industrial than medieval—but there was no question about the room's intended use. Whips, chains, and other items he didn't want to identify hung on hooks or sat on shelves. There were benches and racks, and the straps weren't padded as they would be with BDSM gear. The wood was bloodstained. And some of that blood was Alfie's.

Fear, pain, and desperation so filled the room that Tobias could smell them, could feel them on his skin like tiny claws.

And there in the middle, gaping, was Snjokarl. He held a sinister-looking metal device in one hand and a screwdriver in the other, as if he'd been adjusting the cursed thing. "How?" he demanded as he dropped both items and reached for the knives at his waist.

Olve raised a finger, mumbled his spell, and... nothing happened. "Oh no," he moaned.

At the same moment, Snjokarl opened his mouth and roared, "Guards!"

And also at the same moment, Alfie hurled himself toward Snjokarl—who now held a pair of wicked-looking blades.

Acting entirely on instinct, Tobias dropped Olve—not gently, due to the rush—and used the advantage of his longer legs and greater weight to catch up to Alfie, shove him aside, and launch himself into Snjokarl. The evil elf fell to the floor, Tobias landing atop him. And the knives were between them, digging deep into Tobias's body.

He didn't feel pain yet, just urgency and purpose. "Alfie! Olve! Come here!" Snjokarl bucked and snarled beneath him, plunging the weapons in deeper and twisting them, but Tobias was too heavy for Snjokarl to dislodge. Just to make sure, Tobias grabbed handfuls of Snjokarl's hair.

There was a lot of noise behind him. Running foot-steps, shouts, clattering metal. He felt his own hot blood between his body and Snjokarl's. His vision dimmed and narrowed and his hands and feet went numb.

But when Alfie wrapped himself halfway around him, Tobias felt that. And there was Olve, clutching Tobias's shoulder.

Tobias gritted his teeth and ordered his stupid head to focus. He mentally highlighted the writhing, grotesque mass of the four of them, hit Control+X and, with his last remaining consciousness, dragged them into another window and hit Control+V.

THERE WAS... a lot of noise.

That was the first thing Tobias was aware of. It wasn't screaming, although some of it sounded like crying. Most of it was simply voices. His not-quite-awake brain realized that he *knew* these voices—and that they were safe voices—so he was content to float just beneath the surface of consciousness, letting the words wash over him.

At some point after that, he felt pain, but it was a dull ache and not alarming. It reminded him of when he'd broken his arm as a boy. Not the initial shock and agony, but the throbbing that came a few days later, when he'd been in a cast for a while and the bones were knitting quickly.

So the pain didn't matter, but the other sensation did: fingers gently carding through his hair, untangling the snarls.

He smelled peppermint. And heard someone humming... *White Christmas*?

Finally, Tobias opened his eyes.

Initially, all he saw was whiteness, which was alarming until he realized he was lying on his back and staring at a ceiling. He turned his head slightly—

"Don't move!" The voice was irritated, bossy, and beloved. "I'm still putting you back together and I don't want you undoing my work."

Fine. Tobias rolled his eyes to the side instead. And there was Alfie frowning down at him.

"You're hurt!" Tobias tried to move but Alfie pinned his shoulders in place.

"I'm not. It's your blood, not mine. And I'm afraid you've ruined the countess's lovely rug." Alfie was smiling fondly.

It took a moment for Tobias to catch up. "We're... at Aunt Virginia's home?"

"That's where you brought us. I didn't want to move you until you were less... perforated. Besides which, we would have struggled to lift you. You are not light as a feather. We'll re-situate you somewhere more comfortable shortly."

"Is Olve—"

"Currently in the kitchen with the countess. I believe she's feeding him bits of leftovers from our lovely dinner. I'm rather sorry I missed the bulk of their reunion, because it was quite emotional. But I was otherwise occupied." Alfie leaned down and kissed the tip of Tobias's nose.

And that was nice, until a stab of panic hit. "Snjokarl—"

"Is, as you say, out of the picture. Permanently." Alfie's wicked grin was beautiful to see.

Tobias relaxed a little more. The floor was hard, even with the cushioning of the rug beneath him, but it was nowhere near as bad as that awful cell. God, he must look terrible. And he must reek! "I shouldn't have brought us here. I could have endangered Aunt Virginia."

"I don't think you made a conscious choice, love. And anyway, she's delighted. To have Olve returned, of course, and to see you back in more or less one piece. But also to be in the middle of an exciting adventure. She's almost giddy with it, and I swear she looks years younger."

Oh. "But why did I bring us here specifically?"

"I suspect because this is where your family is."

Family. Right now, that sounded like one of the world's best words.

Tobias wanted to reach up and stroke Alfie's face, but that could wait. "What's next, then?"

"You let me finish healing you. Then I'll see if I can help Olve get back into proper physical shape as well. We all get cleaned up. And then, my dearest, we sit down for a proper celebration. Did you know we were absent from this world for less than a day? Time does such odd things."

"So today...." Tobias thought about it for a moment. "Today is Christmas."

"Indeed."

Tobias thought back on all the holidays he'd spent

with his mother and Aunt Virginia, surrounded by their care. And then the ones where he'd been alone, telling himself the lie that he didn't mind. He was a troll, large and awkward and weird. And that was absolutely fine. Now he had the promise of family and friendship and love. He smiled at the thought that he'd be spending his holidays with his very own beloved Christmas elf.

EPILOGUE

ne year later.

"You taste like a candy cane." To illustrate his point—or really, just because he wanted to—Tobias licked Alfie's ribs.

Alfie, who was often ticklish, wiggled and laughed. "Keep doing that and I might fear that you're trying to eat me up."

"I already did," replied Tobias smugly. "Once last night and then again—"

"I remember the events quite fondly. You needn't remind me."

Tobias laughed and snuggled up against his husband's smooth, strong body. Alfie *did* taste like peppermint, and it wasn't because of the soap they used. His skin temperature was always a little cooler than a human's, which was heavenly in summer and also nice in winter, considering that Tobias tended to run hot. Also his hair was like watered silk, his lips were never chapped, and he had the most adorable dimples right—

"Tobias. Don't you think we ought to get out of bed? We're expected for dinner." Alfie sounded on the verge of laughter, which in turn made Tobias chuckle.

"I don't think they believed us when we said we needed a nap."

Alfie touched the tip of Tobias's nose. "Did you believe them when they said *they* needed their naps?"

"Alfie! Surely you can't believe that— She's in her nineties!"

"But she seems to be enjoying a second flush of youth."

That was undeniably true. Tobias had wondered whether it was due to magic or simply being reunited with her long-lost love, but then he had decided it didn't matter. Aunt Virginia was clearly happy. She'd filled her closet with new clothes, and she and Olve frequented the opera, theatres, museums, and restaurants. They both found it amusing to watch people's reactions to them as a couple: a man seemingly young enough to be the elegant woman's grandson.

Anyway, thinking about his godmother's sex life killed Tobias's amorous mood, so he sighed and rolled out of bed. Alfie ogled him before following suit, and then they teasingly jockeyed for space in the en suite as they washed up. While they dressed, they discussed a couple of highlights from the past year, including Tobias's relief that there had been no troll corpses when they returned to the house in Portland.

Alfie put on an outfit that Tobias had sewn him for special occasions: shiny gold tights and a forest-green tunic with gold embroidery. Alfie had even found pointy-toed slippers, also in gold and green. He said it was the sort of thing he would have worn to a semi-formal occasion at the castle, although he chose to forego the traditional peaked cap.

As for Tobias, he donned a pair of nice khakis, a white button-down shirt, and a blue tie embroidered with white snowflakes. Alfie had seen the tie a month earlier and insisted that Tobias buy it.

Tobias thought that he looked plain and boring compared to his husband, but Alfie's eyes shone when he looked at him. And Alfie always seemed to be telling the truth when he said that Tobias was beautiful.

Aunt Virginia and Olve had redecorated over the past months, so all the rooms were fresh and bright, and her first husband's paintings carefully hung. For today, Olve had also added several dozen small shiny balls that hung from the ceiling without visible support and slowly twirled, making the light dance and glitter. Together with the winter greenery and flowers arranged around the room, the effect was enchanting, like stepping into fairyland.

But honestly, Tobias's entire life seemed enchanted nowadays.

He and Alfie were still admiring the effect when Aunt Virginia made her grand entrance, as she liked to do. Her tea-length cocktail dress was iceberg-blue with a glittery lace bodice and a flared skirt, and her hair—naturally white—was done up in an elegant arrangement.

"My Lady." Alfie executed a deep bow. "Are you the Countess of Contovello or the Snow Queen?"

She waved a hand. "I'm your Aunt Virginia." But she looked pleased.

"You do look amazing," agreed Tobias.

Before she could pretend to fend off the compliments, Olve appeared, dressed in a good but entirely ordinary suit. He was slightly plump now, with rounded cheeks and eyes that often lingered on his wife. His smile rarely faded. "I hope you've worked up an appetite," he announced, winking broadly, which made Tobias blush.

Then, at Olve's insistence, everyone else sat and he started toting in food from the kitchen. It had turned out that he loved to cook and, for that matter, to serve. "A good meal is the best kind of magic," he liked to say.

It was a feast. There were two kinds of salads, turkey baked in puff pastry, along with cranberries and hazelnuts, glazed carrots, and crusty brown bread. It was all perfectly delicious, and the conversation flowed like good wine. Olve and Aunt Virginia spoke of some recent museum exhibits and of their planned springtime trip to Italy. Tobias and Alfie talked about some of the renovations they were doing on their Portland bungalow. Last year's fight with the trolls had caused some property damage, which provided a good excuse to finally restore the woodwork and floors to their original state.

"One more piece of good news," Tobias announced as they drank tea and ate spiced cardamom cookies. "Alfie's going to enroll in the community college next semester."

Aunt Virginia clapped her hands. "How lovely! Do you have a plan of study in mind, dear?"

Uncharacteristically, Alfie looked a bit shy. He was still getting used to the concept that he had value even though he was no longer a prince. "I, er, I was thinking of becoming a nurse. My healing skills are all well and good, but I think that science would be helpful as well."

Tobias reached over to squeeze his hand. He was so damned proud of his husband, who'd adapted to an entirely new world with enthusiasm and grace.

Olve nodded. "Remember, magic *is* science—it simply hasn't been studied properly to find out how it works. I'm doing a bit of that myself and, Tobias, perhaps later we can discuss some software to help me. Alfie, I'm certain you'll make an excellent nurse."

Of course he would. What patient wouldn't be cheered by Alfie's charm and soothed by his kindness? Whenever Tobias had a frustrating day at work or felt awkward in a social situation, all he needed was a smile from his husband or a gentle touch, and his mood immediately brightened.

"How about you, Toby?" asked Aunt Virginia softly. "Do you have any special plans for the coming year?"

"To support Alfie and be happy together. And maybe have a small adventure or two with him. You know, YOLO and all." He grinned at her.

And that was it. He had all he needed: family, friends, and love. His heart was so full it was a wonder it still fit in his chest.

As the conversation continued around him, he looked up at the shelf next to the dining room door. Arranged there carefully were the porcelain elves with their skis and their bags full of gifts. They looked merry.

But their companion looked considerably less happy.

Sitting on the shelf beside them was an elf doll with brown hair, lavender eyes, and a decidedly sour expression. Its Christmasy tunic and hose bordered on garish, and its pointy hat was slightly too small. Tobias gave the doll an evil trollish grin.

Then he squeezed his beloved's hand, put another few cookies on his plate, and listened to Aunt Virginia tell a scandalous, hilarious tale about her third husband, the movie star.

This was easily his best holiday so far. With, he knew, many more to come.

SHELF-MADE MAN

ABOUT THE AUTHOR

Kim Fielding is very pleased every time someone calls her eclectic. Winner of the BookLife Prize for Fiction, a Lambda Award finalist and a Foreword INDIE finalist, she has migrated back and forth across the western two-thirds of the United States and, after a long exile, has recently returned to Portland, Oregon. She's a university professor who dreams of being able to travel and write full time. She also dreams of having two daughters who fully appreciate her, a husband who isn't obsessed with football, and a house that cleans itself. Some dreams are more easily obtained than others.

Kim can be found on her blog: http:// kfieldingwrites.com/

Facebook: https://www.facebook.com/KFielding Writes

and Twitter: @KFieldingWrites

Her e-mail is kim@kfieldingwrites.com

ALSO BY KIM FIELDING

Staged

Rattlesnake

Astounding!

Motel. Pool.

The Tin Box

Venetian Masks

Brute

Novellas

Shelf Made Man

Man of His Dreams

Bread Crumbs

Regifted

Bite Me: An Elucidation in Three Acts

Farkas

Ash Believes the Impossible

A Very Genre Christmas

Gravemound

The Solstice Kings

Dei Ex Machina

The Golem of Mala Lubovnya

Refugees

The Dance

Transformation

Summerfield's Angel

The Tale of August Hayling

Phoenix

Grown-Up

The Pillar

The Border

Housekeeping

Night Shift

Speechless

Guarded

The Downs

Short Stories and Collections

Dog Days of December

Firestones

Dreidels and Do-Overs

Get Lit

Christmas Present

Act One and Other Stories

Exit through the Gift Shop

Dear Ruth

Grateful

The Sacrifice and Other Stories

Saint Martin's Day

The Festivus Miracle

Joys R Us

Alaska

A Great Miracle Happened There

Violet's Present

Standby

Anyplace Else